3 Way Love

In the town of Humble, California, it is in a word, utopia. It's all-year-round summer, meaning it's sunny all-year-round. Isn't it fantastic?! Not only that, its in close proximity to Los Angeles, the land of glam and heartbreak. The land of mistrust and deceit and lies. The land where everybody wants a piece of the action.

In Humble, everybody accepts everybody else, no matter race, sexuality or gender. Everybody is equal in his/her own way. There is no such thing as status quo.

This is a town where money *does* grow on trees. At the beginning of each and every month, the good citizens of Humble miraculously received $100,000 in cold, hard cash. Yep they *sure* live the good life. They live in the lap of luxury. Nobody knows who or where the money comes from. With the money, nobody has to work, ever again.

Besides nobody *needs* to work anyway. Everything is pretty much run by technology. All anybody ever does is hang out, live life and have a good time

♥

♥   ♥

Aileen 'Ally' Wang is all about hearts and angels and butterflies, oh my! But she is a tomboy at heart. The way she sees it, she's a tomboy for life! Being the youngest of five siblings-all of 'em boys-can do that to a girl.

Aileen loves to grab life by the reins and never let go. She lives life to the fullest-to the extreme, quite literally! She likes extreme sports,

1

Connie Cyndi Chu

no *likes* isn't the word for it; it's more like *love*. Whenever she takes up an extreme sport, she often throws all caution to the wind. She always says, "Remember, no pain, no gain!" is something her eldest brother Aaron, who is a professional X-treme sports athlete, always, says to her. Another brother is a stuntman for the movie stars.

Along with being down on X-treme sports, she likes being a daredevil. She has done, to name a few, rock climbing-real rock climbing, not those faux ones they have in those rock-climbing gyms. She has also done skydiving. Oh, it was helleva rush! The adrenaline was incredible. She wouldn't stop talking about it for days after! She has also tried hang gliding, windsurfing, and bungee jumping. She did bungee jumping to get over her fear of heights. Oh yeah, baby it has been one trill-ride after another. Her main goal in life is to be a professional daredevil. She has an interest in motorcross racing because one of her brother, Cal, is a professional racer; he wins just about every single race he participates in.

Oh the guys envy her and the girls are so jealous of her, they couldn't see straight. The guys are envious of her because she is breaking the gender barrier while the girls are jealous of her because they want to be like her; they look up to her. Granted, they admire her for her ambitious quality.

One thing that is not so very admirable is she that she sleeps around with not just guys but girls too. But not with her usual crowd, so no one who knows her well knows that she sleeps around with both guys and dolls. Only her best friend, Jasmine 'Jazz' Angel, knows that she is a bisexual.

Jasmine and Ally, who have been the best of friends since they were in diapers-they even shared the same playpen-have lots in common. They do all these crazy, X-treme sports together. If Aileen is doing her latest sport, whatever it may be, Jasmine is usually there with her, picking up the pieces, quite literally. If Aileen gets injured, Jasmine takes her to the ER. They have been through thick and thin, through good and bad. They are the best of the best. Ally's single mother threw her out of their scanty apartment when she found out she was sleeping around with not only guys but girls too, Jasmine was there. Jasmine is only one who knows that Aileen is bisexual, but Aileen doesn't know Jasmine's secret: she hasn't come out of the closet yet as a lesbian. She doesn't want to come out because she's afraid her parents will reject her like Jasmine's mother did to her.

Fickle as she is, Aileen bed-hops, having one sexual encounter almost every night, not knowing whom she spends the night with. Either she's too drunk because she lost a race or a bet or too wild and crazy to care if she won a race or a bet. Some weeks she doesn't even goes home with someone. If she gets too drunk, she calls for back up in the form of Jasmine, no questions asked.

Their mutual friend, Robyn Wright, who runs an online matchmaking service, decides to hook 'em up. Jasmine secretly confides in Robyn that she might have a crush on Aileen. So Robyn plays matchmaker with the two best friends.

If it's any coincidence, Jasmine and Aileen have the same day off, so Robyn decides to set 'em up on a blind date.

"Hi Aileen," Robyn said. "This is Robyn. How are you?"

"I'm fine, thanks. Robyn," Aileen replied. "So what's going on?'

"How would you like to go on a blind date?" Robyn asked.

"With whom, may I asked?" wondered Aileen.

"Uh-uh," admonished Robyn. "Can't tell you that. Otherwise, it would ruin the surprise."

Aileen said, "What should I wear for the blind date to recognize me?"

Connie Cyndi Chu

"Hm," Robyn said thoughtfully. "How about your red floral scarf?"

"Thanks for setting this up for me, Robyn. I love you, dearest," Aileen said, getting ready to hang up.

"You're welcome."

♥

♥   ♥

"Hi, dear Jasmine," Robyn greeted her friend. "How are doing today? Everything okay?"

"Yes, everything is going rather well for me, " Jasmine replied. "How about you?"

"Have I a treat for you!" Robyn exclaimed. "I got you a blind date, girl! Are you excited or what!

"Wow, cool," Jasmine said "I'm *so* there! You are the best!"

"Thanks! You're not so bad yourself! Just remember to have a good time! Oh, yeah, before I forget, wear your blue knit hat!"

"Will do!"

"Have a good time!"

"Thanks for setting it up and everything! Love ya! Call ya tomorrow with the deets!"

♥   ♥

♥

Planet Angel Dee-lite!

The ladies are supposed to meet at Twinkieware, a local teen hangout for people 25 and under. That night, when Jasmine spots Aileen's red floral scarf, she realizes it is her very best friend, Aileen.

"Hi there," Aileen said.

"Hey, Ally," Jasmine greeted her BFF. "What's up?"

"I'm here to meet my blind date." Aileen said quizzically. "Is it you?"

"I guess so," Jasmine replied.

"But you're straight," said Aileen.

"Wanna know a secret?" Jasmine said.

"Do tell."

"I'm a lesbian," Jasmine. "Now no one but you can know about this, okay?"

"Sure, I swear I won't tell anyone," Aileen said. "I'll take it to the grave if I have to."

"You came up with this blind date idea, and put Robyn up to it, didn't you?"

"I didn't know it was you who was my blind date, I swear it," Jasmine protested.. "I swear it. Honest to God. I didn't know."

"Okay, okay, I believe you," Aileen relented. "I was just teasing. God, you can't even take a joke."

"I love you, not as just a friend or even as a friend with benefits but as something more."

"I never knew you felt this way," Aileen said huskily, caressing Jasmine's cheek with the back of her hand. "I love you too. You're my guardian angel."

And with that, they kiss. They have a girl-on-girl liplock. They have a long, lingering French kiss. Their tongues entangle together. The

5

world, as they know it, disappear from them. The two ladies kissing didn't cause a stir because nobody cares or flinches. To other people, they are just two lovelorn, crazy-in-love lovebirds. Ah, the innocence of love!

Just then, some perfect stranger, a total, complete stranger comes into Twinkieware. A hot, hunky, muscular, well-tanned man with an exceptional abfab surfer bod with a six-pack and with his dark blond hair, he looks like he has just finished surfing since he's carrying a wet surfboard. All he's wearing is boy shorts that show off his strong, muscular legs. The stranger must be new to town because he keeps looking around for a waiter or a counterperson, but there ain't any; just a kiosk to order food from.

On top of the kiosks, there is a sign that says, **Food Rack** in bold letterings. He scans the menu over and over but couldn't find tea-he searches high n' lo so he ends up ordering coffee. The coffee comes down through a dumbwaiter.

Aileen and Jasmine pull away long enough to see the stranger come into Twinkieware and order his coffee. One look at him, Aileen falls madly, deeply, head-over-heels in love with him. She feels her heart skip a beat upon seeing him. Her stomach is doing flip-flops, starting to have butterflies, something she never have before when she first sees a man. It is love at first sight! Ah love at first sight! How infinitely possible!

"Jazz, excuse me for a moment," Aileen said.

Without waiting for a response from Jasmine, Aileen slithers away. She goes straight up to the stranger and said, "Never seen you around these parts before. Are you new here?"

"Yes," the stranger said. "My name's Chase Montgomery. Friends called me Monty. What's yours?" holding his hand out to shake.

"Aileen," Aileen said. "Aileen Wang. Friends called me Ally," taking his hand to shake.

"Nice to finally see a friendly face," Chase said. "I thought this town was devoid of people."

"No way," Aileen said. "Though it sometimes seems that way, huh? Hey, Monty, why don't you come and meet my friend?"

"Hey Jazz," Aileen called to Jasmine. "C'mere for a sec, I want you to meet someone."

Jasmine thought, *Oh great, another day, another conquest. This guy's here to ruin my date with Aileen.*

Jasmine comes grudgingly dragging her feet at a snail's pace. Meanwhile, Aileen feels pride in Jasmine and is telling Chase all of her virtues to him.

"...she's the best friend a girl could have."

By this time, Jasmine has made it to their sides. Jasmine thought, *She still thinks of me as her best friend.*

There are introductions all around, starting with Jasmine.

"Here she is," Aileen said. "Jazz, my best friend," motioning to Jasmine. "And here is Monty," motioning to Chase, "who's new in town."

"Hey, Monty," Aileen said. "Since you're new here, why don't we show you around town?"

"Count me out," Jasmine said quickly.

"Why?" Aileen asked.

As if you didn't know, thought Jasmine snidely. *Ruined our date, Monty, you jerk.*

"I don't want to be a bother," Jasmine said.

"Oh, it's no bother," Aileen said.

"I'm going home." Jasmine said.

"Oh just leave her alone," Chase said.

7

Connie Cyndi Chu

So they go their separate ways: Aileen and Chase go on a tour of Humble while Jasmine goes home to cut her losses. She decides to try again with Aileen some other time because with Aileen it always ends up being a one-night stand when it comes to other homo sapiens, especially strangers.

♥

♥   ♥

The next afternoon, Aileen calls Jasmine up. "You'll never believe where I am in a million years!"

"Oh, man," said Jasmine groggily. "What time is it? Oh, my God it's nearly noon!"

"Never mind that," Aileen said excitedly. "I'm at Chase's private cabin in the woods! His family is incredibly loaded! Man, oh, man, I can't get over it!"

` Jasmine is less than trilled since she thinks that Aileen would've left Chase in the dust. Jasmine wants Aileen for herself.

"That's great, Ally." Jasmine said nonchalantly and as calmly as she could.

"And get this, Jazz," Aileen said excitedly. "His family owns half of Hollywood Hills!"

"What do you mean, he has his own private cabin? Doesn't he shares it with his family?"

"No, every member of his family has their own private cabin. Isn't it great?"

"Cool, I always knew you would find your soulmate one of these days, Ally." Jasmine said, not really meaning it.

♥
♥   ♥

Days later, a glowing Jasmine comes back to Humble. The second she reaches town, she goes directly to Aileen's house to apologize for cutting their date short when she first saw Chase.

"Hi hon," Aileen said. "Before you say anything, I want to apologize for the other day for running out on you. I totally don't deserve you as a friend."

"Oh, it's okay," said Jasmine. "No need to apologize. So welcome back. How was your getaway with Monty?"

"It was simply divine!" exclaimed Aileen, spinning around with her arms around herself. "He was so nice and warm. We cuddle and made love till daylight!"\

♥
♥   ♥

After Aileen leaves, Jasmine begins to plot how to get Aileen. She is no competition to the poor lil rich boy, Chase Montgomery. But she figures, if she proves she can be just as romantic as he is to Aileen, then she would want her.

She decides to prepare a home cook romantic meal with candelights and everything. She feels love is in the air. Ah the magic is in the air!

9

Connie Cyndi Chu

The minute Aileen arrives for their romantic dinner, she thinks it is just a friendly get-together but boy, is she in for a surprise! She doesn't know what Jasmine has in store for both of them tonight.

As Aileen gets settled into the loveseat, Jasmine gets her a bottle of wine to relax her.

"Here you go, Ally." Jasmine said. "Red wine. A toss to us."

"To our friendship, Jazz." Aileen said.

"Yes, to our friendship," said Jasmine through gritted teeth, cringing on the inside, clinking glasses. "I'll be right back," said Jasmine, jumping up. I've made *all* your favorites."

"Do you any help?"

"No thanks. You're my guest tonight. I won't allow it. Relax, get comfortable, and put your feet up."

While Aileen relaxes in the living room, turning on the TV (mind you, they've been to each other houses a million times already), Jasmine goes back in the kitchen to finish up with their meal. With the meal preparations underway, Jasmine is practically giddy with joy! She is, to say to the least, overcome with emotion! Tears of happiness are pouring down her face. Quickly she wipes them away with the back of her hand. Of the duo, she is always known as the more emotional one while Aileen is the headstrong one. Aileen can't see the preps being made because French doors connect to the living room and dining room. Jasmine sets all the food on the table. Then she puts two tall white candlesticks in a silver candlestick holder and lights it with a lighter. Blowing the light out from the lighter, she sees that the preparations are marvelous, just *marvcelous*!

"Okay, ready!" Jasmine called, opening the wide French doors. "Come n' get it!"

"Oh my gosh," Aileen gasped when she enters the dining area. "I didn't know it is a romantic dinner; I thought it is just a friendly get-together."

Jasmine looks crestfallen. Like the best friend Aileen is, she notices it right away.

"Remember the other night when we were French-kissing?" asked Jasmine. "We could try it again. We could talk till the sun comes up and then some. *But no talking about Monty.* I could *not* stress it enough. Tonight's our night to be together."

"You're serious about this, aren't you?" Aileen asked her best friend.
"Oh yeah," replied Jasmine.

"Okay, I'll give us a chance," agreed Aileen.

"Now, please, sit down. Our dinner's getting cold."

As soon as the ladies sit down, Jasmine notices Aileen's honey brown eyes sparkling with anticipation. It is probably the candles, but it calls for a compliment.

"Your eyes are radiant. They're positively glowing. Fact: your whole face is glowing."

"Aw shucks," Aileen said. "It's just the candles."

"No, I mean it. You look really awesome tonight," said Jasmine.

"That's 'cause I met the man of my dreams," said Aileen, swooning. "Oh sorry, we said we weren't gonna talk about Monty.

As they eat their lasagna, they are both deep in thought.

Why is this guy coming out of nowhere and claiming her just like that? thought Jasmine enviously.

I'm so in love; I can't possibly hide any longer, thought Aileen. *But what is Jazz up to? I thought it was just a casual dinner between*

11

Connie Cyndi Chu

friends, thinking back to the last few days before Chase *rudely* interrupted their dinner, remembering that Jasmine came out to her at Twinkieware. *Oh my god, Jazz is a lesbian and* so *wants me!* coming to the full realization. *How thoughtless of me! I've should've known better than to show off my affection for Monty, but she's been my best friend all my life... my* only *best friend. And now this*, berating herself for her selfishness. *I'll make a more conscious effort to be more intimate with her*, she vowed.

"Jazz, I love you as more than a friend. I love you til the world ends. You're my anchor and I'm your rock. I love you," said Aileen, reaching over across the table to squeeze her hands and give it a quick kiss on the back.

"Oh Ally, I love you too," Jasmine said. "You don't know how long I've waited for you to hear you say that."

But while Jasmine is saying this, Aileen is planning how to use Jasmine, *I'll be intimate with her, all right. I'll use her as my friend with benefits.* After dinner, they have each other for dessert. They cuddle and make out on the loveseat. They *sure* did a lot of French-kissing, entangling their tongues together. After drinking nearly the whole bottle of red wine, they get fairly loaded.

They get hot n' heavy physically. On the way to Jasmine's massive bedroom, they are practically taking each other's clothes off while kissing passionately nonstop as if the fever will stop. By the time they reach Jasmine's huge red king-sized bed (romantic, ain't it?) they have taken each other's clothes off and are having hot and heavy sex.

After they have full-on sex, they are spent. Exhausted, they sleep for an hour or something like that.

They moan and groan as they continue their high-energy kinky sex.

"Oh, baby," Aileen moaned. "This is the thing."

"Oooh yea," Jasmine groaned. "I…love...you."

"Give it to me, baby," Aileen moaned.

Then they decide to have kinky sex.

"I've got a gift for you. Would you mind trying it on?"

"Oh a present for me?" Aileen said. "You shouldn't have."

So Aileen goes to the bathroom to put on the leather outfit. Quickly Jasmine changes into a tight spandex bodysuit-a form-fitting number that wraps around her curvaceous body-the kind dancers use for dancing-only thing is she doesn't wear tights; she wears fishnet stockings. It is what you might call a stripper's outfit. Underneath her spandex bodysuit, she is in the nude. When Aileen comes out, she is wearing a dominatrix outfit complete with a whip and a pair of handcuffs in a side holster.

"C'mon, Jazzie," said Aileen huskily. "Get on the bed," hitting the whip smack-dab on the floor. "I got handcuffs."

"Oh, you look so totally awesome, Ally!" Jasmine exclaimed. "Lovin' it! Lovin' it!"

"You don't look so bad yourself," Aileen said.

"You are a dog, Jazzie," Aileen said. "You need to be spanked," and with that she whips Jasmine's behind, surprise at how strong she is. Jasmine is on all fours, trying to escape from Aileen's ambush. "Now grovel at my feet, you dog," Aileen taunted Jasmine. "Get into the bed."

Aileen then strips off all her clothes on the spot, leaving her whip on the ground, bringing the handcuffs to the bed with her so that she could cuff Jasmine to the headboard and have raunchy sex.

"Ooh," Aileen said, who is on top, pulling off Jasmine's bodysuit by hand. "Oh, yea."

"Aah," Jasmine said, jerking upward with each groan and moan.

After they grow exhausted from sex, they fall asleep in each other's arms.

13

Connie Cyndi Chu

♥ ♥
♥

In the wee hours of the morning, Aileen slips out of Jasmine's place quietly since she has to meet up with Monty for breakfast before he goes play golf with some friends. But first, she has to get home to change. Also, she doesn't want Jasmine to know she's still seeing Chase after the night they have together.

By the time she reaches the Hollywood Hills, where Chase lives in a gated community, to change it is now dawn. (Within days of knowing Chase, she has moved in with him.) She takes a quick shower, changes into nice clothes. (It wouldn't do to wear clothes from the night before. Even though she wasn't with Chase last night, she knows herself her clothes are from the night before.)

Aileen and Chase meet for breakfast at the Hollywood Hills Country Club. She spots him right away, waiting for her patiently with his golf clubs in their bag by his side.

"Hi, m' love," said Aileen, kissing Chase on the cheek gently.

"G'morning, darling," said Chase, turning to kiss fully. "Where were you last night?"

"I spent the night with my best friend," said Aileen. "Don't freak," seeing Chase's expression turns worried. "We slept in separate beds; we've had a slumber party-we always have done that," Aileen fibbed.

"Oh," Chase relaxed. "If that's what it is. But I heard rumors floating around that you're bi. Is it true?"

"No, but what if it is, would you *still* accept me?"

"I need time to think it through," Chase said. "Let's just get through this meal together, okay? I gotta meet my friends at the golf course."

"One more thing: are you open to open relationships?"

"Sure, why not? It's the 21st century."

"Now I've gotta hurry, have to meet my friends at the golf course."

They hurriedly finish their breakfast, and then they are off. Even though Aileen doesn't like to play golf, she does like to watch her man golf. She already has met all his friends because he is one of the most popular member of the country club.

By the time they reach the golf course, (Yup, they have their own caddies.) most of Chase's friends and GFs have already gotten there. The GFs come to give their guys morale support. While the men play golf, the ladies watch on the sidelines. After they tee off, Chase is off to a good start. They ladies follow the guys from hole to hole with Chase ahead. (He is flawless in every sport known to man. He's da man! Being a natural-born athlete, he wins every time, so he never needs to practice.) With three more holes to go, he is winning, without a doubt. At last, they finally reach the last hole, winning ahead by one measly point! Yay!

They all troop back to the country club to celebrate.

"Drinks are on me," called out Chase. "Celebration's on the house."

After giving his credit card to the bartender, he said to Chase, "You may be our best customer yet, but your credit card's all maxed out. Sorry," giving Chase's credit card back to him.

"Put on my tab!" yelled Chase. "Y' know I'm good for it!"

He has to yell because the country club has loud dance music playing whenever there's some sort of celebration.

"Can we go somewhere quiet and talk?" Aileen texted Chase.

"Sure, " Chase texted back

Connie Cyndi Chu

So they leave the bar/restaurant area of the country club unnoticed for a nearby park, leaving Chase's friends behind, who are drinking shotglass of tequila after shotglass.

The local park, Humble Park, is a small area with greenery and tall pine trees that give off the pine scent in the air with rocks of every size and shape and benches for sitting and daydreaming the day away. You can hear birds chirping, but you can't see 'em. It's got numerous of flowers of every single type. It is also got a cool 52-foot long creek with a cool working spinning sawmill. Also known as Kissing Creek, it is a hot spot for local teens to come here and neck and make out at night.

Aileen and Chase come here every single time after Chase wins a sports event, which is practically every time. Oh yea, she has picked a winner, all right!

"Congrats on your win," said Aileen laying a wet one on him enveloping him in a huge bear hug, wrapping her arms around his neck as he wraps his arms around her waist.

" Thanks," said Chase.

"You said earlier that you believe in open relationship."

"Yes, I said that," agreed Chase. "Hypothetically speaking."

"What if?" hesitated Aileen.

"Yes?"

"What if we have an open relationship?" Aileen asked. "Would you want to?"

"But I thought you want to date exclusively."

"I thought so too," Aileen said, averting her glance. "But then something happened."

"What happened?"

"Promise not to get mad?"

"I swear."

"Remember how I told you earlier I wasn't bi?"

"Yes?" Chase said, then it dawns on him. "You are bi, then?"

"Yup, without a doubt," Aileen confessed, feeling vulnerable. "I can't help the way I am."

"No, you can't," said Chase, taking pity on her. "I love you. Y'know that, don't you? Of course, I'll allow you to have an open relationship with anyone of your desired."

Aileen's eyes were brimming with tears. She is ecstatic that Chase didn't get mad and that he allows her to have an open relationship.

♥

♥   ♥

With that, they goes back to his penthouse to make sweet, sweet love. It isn't the first time she has ever been in his penthouse, but it looks really gorgeous today.

When they get to his front entrance of his penthouse, it is decorated with trellis of faux leaves bordering the entryway He carries her over the threshold like a married couple. Lovely, ain't it? They are in the mood for hot, tempestuous sex. Practically every time he wins a game or something like that, he would take her back to his penthouse and make sweet, sweet love; it doesn't matter whether it's day or night. As soon as they cross the treshold, they saw rose petals on the ground leading all the way to the bedroom. So romantic, isn't it?

"Oh Monty," whispered Aileen. "You're such a romantic."

17

Connie Cyndi Chu

"I love you." Said Chase huskily. "You're my one true love."

"I love you too."

They walk into his bedroom, which is opened by French doors. It is filled with candles. On the foot stand by the bed is a wrapped gift, which Chase hands to Aileen.

"For you, Aileen, my girl. Go on and change into it. Don't be bashful now."

So she goes into the bathroom and unwraps the gift. It turns out to be a red silk lace teddy from, duh, Victoria's Secret. And she admires herself, yea, she's vain, in the full-length mirror every which way, and likes what she sees before stepping out of the bathroom to show off to Chase, who is lounging on the bed when she comes out.

"Ooh, baby," Chase whistled a catcall. "You look deee-licious. Come get some sugar from your sugar daddy," pulling her towards him so that they have a long, lingering, melt-in-your-mouth kiss.

"Why don't you do some pole dancing?" Chase asked Aileen. "You know I like that."

So she did some pole dancing on the pole he had installed after he found out she was a former dancer. It was very seductive like a stripper. Holding the pole with her hands and wrapping her legs around the pole, she pulls back and swings, round and round, she goes till there's no end.

"Oh yea," Chase, "Give it to me, baby!"

. She is totally in the moment. The world has fallen away. Only she exists. She is in the zone. She is getting hotter and hotter and hotter till she couldn't take it anymore. She is feeling so sensuous So intoxicating. Oh, so hot.

By then, both of 'em are hot n' bothered, so Aileen stops pole dancing and climbs into bed with Chase to make sweet lovin' all day and all night long.

♥

♥

♥

♥

Quietly Aileen steals away into the early dawn light to her fire engine red convertible. (Yea, Chase brought it for her for their first month anniversary together as a couple.) She goes to Jasmine's house to surprise her before she leaves for a day of sunbathing.

"Hey Jazz," Aileen said.

"Hey Ally," Jasmine said.

"That was some night we had the other night, wasn't it?"

"It sure was!" Aileen said. "Listen, we need to talk."

"About what?"

"About our relationship."

"Yea, what about it?"

"Do you consider our relationship a sexual relationship or a friendship?" asked Aileen.

"We could be friends with benefits," replied Jasmine.

"How about an open relationship?" asked Aileen. "Would you want an open relationship?"

"Sure, why not? It's the 21st century. I can't say I didn't think about it. It's a possibility," replied Jasmine.

"Cool."

♥   ♥

♥   ♥

Connie Cyndi Chu

The trio decides to finally meet one another, arrange by Aileen as a couple At long last, they shall meet face-to-face-to-face. The reception is, to say the least, well received. Everybody likes each other. Aileen agrees to do *all* the talking.

"Hi Monty," said Aileen, kissing her BF on the cheek. "Remember meeting one another?"

"Hi, nice seeing again," said Chase, shaking Jasmine's hand.

"Likewise."

"You both agree to be part of an open relationship, right?"

Both Chase and Jasmine nod their heads.

"And I'm gonna be the liaison between the two of you guys," continued Aileen, feeling like she has just made a sexual conquest. In a way, she did. "So let's start the games begin!"

"Cheers to new beginnings!" Aileen said, raising her glass.

"Cheers!" They clinked glasses.

"Another round!" yelled Chase.

Barbie & Ken: The Untold Story

Note: Enter BarbieWorld, where everything is materialistic and fake like mainstream pop culture.

Barbie and Ken Dall are the latest Hollywood "It" couple of the 21st century! To what do we owe this honor, you say?

Well, besides Barbie being a typical girly girl who has a mean tomboyish streak since she grew up among boys being the only girl in the family, she knows how to pull a prank or two on boys and has an undying love for sports. But she still loves to dress up-she calls it 'playing dress up,' looking for hotties cause she wanted to blend in with her gal pals in her hot pink convertible; the license of her convertible has her name on it. She loves to think the best in people.

To look the perfect size 0, she has gone on crash diets, which includes taking diet pills. She has an eating disorder. She has gone from a size 4 to a size 0 but at what cost? All her life growing up, her family, friends, even her peers told her she needed plastic surgery. She has had everything imaginable-you name it, she done it.

But since marrying her lifelong boyfriend, Ken, six months ago, she has devoted all her time to him and their 2.5 children (actually 2 children). I know this may be a little old-fashioned, but she is a stay-at-home mom while Ken brings home the bacon.

All of a sudden, one day, while talking on the phone with her BFF, Stacy (short for Anastasia) put the thought in her head that she should do something more with her life like get a job or give back to the community.

Stacy calls her everyday just to pester her, but today Barbie could really used the pick-me-up since she's been so depressed lately ever since she lost her position as a teacher aide at her youngest's preschool.

"Don't you feel claustrophobic sometimes?" asked Stacy who works as an accountant.

"Yes, I do. But what can I do?"

"Why don't you go look for a job on Craigslist or something? Volunteer at Bunny's (the youngest) school. I don't know."

"Okay, I will do just that!" exclaimed Barbie.

"Atta girl!" Stacy praised. "Tell about it when you get back."

Several days later, Barbie got a job! But instead of using her first name on her application, which she knows people won't take seriously, she decides to use her middle name, Candice. She decides not to use her last name either; she uses her mother's maiden name, which is Hart. In the professional world, she is now known as Candice Hart. Her husband, Ken, is displeased with this when he finds out. When he finds out, there is hell to pay.

"Why did you take your middle name and your mother's maiden name?"

"I thought it would be more professional that way," Barbie said meekly.

"Are you ashamed of me? Is that it?" yelled Ken.

"Don't be that way, Ken," said Barbie soothingly, trying to placate him. "You know I love you."

"Well I don't feel the love right now," Ken said, keeping his cool, taking his jacket out of the closet and walking out of the door.

What have I done? commiserated Barbie, twisting a ringlet of platinum blonde hair around her finger. *All my life I tried to be prefect, but where does that get me? Nowhere! I guess beauty is only skin deep after all.*

Barbie decides to call her BFF, Stacy for advice. She calls up Stacy, who is with her boyfriend Ranger, at the moment, in tears. They are sleeping together in their penthouse after having full-on sex when she receives the call from Barbie.

"K-k-k-Ken- he walked out on me," gasped Barbie by this time in hysterics

23

"Slow down, girl," advised Stacy. "Do you want me to come over?"

"What's wrong *now?*" mumbled Ranger in his sleep.

They are both used to these calls by now. Barbie and Ken aren't all that cookie-cutter, picture-perfect as a couple. What lies beneath that entire perfect exterior is a lot of messed-up craziness in that marriage. Only close friends and family know about the trials and tribulations they go through. Although they're famous (make that infamous), they have no qualms about being on a reality show; only thing is they hate the media and how they'll be judged if they were to be on a reality show.

Stacy comes over to Barbie's Malibu condo she share with Ken but since Ken is probably out busily getting drunk at some dive bar, she's safe from his violent temper. And you *don't* want to be around when he comes home drunk.

Before he fell into a deep depression over losing his job of 5 years, on his downtime, he would go surfing. Tall, lean, muscular with a surfer's body, he has sun-bleached blond hair and a carefree attitude about life. Being born with a silver spoon in his mouth, he worked very little until his parents cut him off over his all-night partying, which consisted of all-night drink binges and doing drugs. His parents gave him many warnings before-there was even an intervention but to no avail. (like 'if you don't shape up, we're gonna cut you off)

After he was cut off, he went into rehab and now he no longer takes drugs. But ever since he was laid off from his job, she has been enabling him, feeding his drinking and drug habit. She gets her money from her very rich parents, the Cues, who have their very own real estate company for the stars. They often said that they're 'the real estate agents to the stars,' selling million, sometimes billion homes a year.

Ever since Ken lost his job at a private, local construction company for faulty wiring nonetheless, he has been taking his anger out on Barbie. He also has been frequenting all these dive bars; every time a different one. By the time he leaves the bar, he is so unwelcome to come back anymore because he is stinking drunk. But Barbie has been tolerating him, listening to him freeload about him losing his job and not being able to go to his parents for money anymore. Now Barbie is at the end of her line.

It has been several months since there has been income coming into the Dalls' home, so it is up to Barbie to get a job.

When Stacy reaches the Dalls residence, she lets herself in. Barbie gives Stacy a key since she helps her through thick and thin and feels she could be trusted.

"What happened, sweetcakes?"

Connie Cyndi Chu

Her maid has moved her from the living room floor to the loveseat, which she is now curled up in a fetal position, crying her eyes out, her makeup streaking down face and making a general mess of the upholstered loveseat.

"She's been cryin' for the last half hour. Poor dear," said her maid Doria. Her maid used to be her nanny. "She's afraid that loser Ken won't come back but come back he will. Probably to wreck havoc on this household."

"Thanks for watching her for me."

"No problem," said Doria. "Your debt is mine. She could be my daughter," leaving the two friends alone.

"C'mon, let's clean you up," said Stacy, pulling Barbie gently to her feet.

As Stacy leads her slowly to the bathroom to wash, she put her arm around her shoulders.

When they return, Barbie is as clean as a whistle physically, but emotionally she is in turmoil. Ken has never laid a hand on her even when he is drunk. He only used horrible words against her, more like verbal abuse, if you want to get technical. He has called her every derogatory name in the book that she lost all of her self-confidence, her self-worth. Even her self-esteem is at an all-time low. Poor thing.

"Why were you crying? What happened?"

"I-I-I g-g-got a job," said Barbie, breaking down again.

"That's good news, isn't it?"

"Y-y-yes, but you haven't heard the worst part: I changed my name. Used my middle name and my mother's maiden name instead of Barbie Dall.

"Oh, I get it," said Stacy, realization dawning in her eyes. "He found out about it and storm off."

"Why don't you come stay at my place for awhile till things cool down? Bring the kids along. They love hanging out at my place."

"They do, don't they? No way am I turning down that job! "

"Who says you have to turn down anything?" said Stacy gently. "All I'm saying is, stay at my place for awhile till things cool down between you and Ken, then if not we'll see how it goes."

"Are you suggesting I dump him?"

"We'll see how it goes," Stacy cajoled.

"All right, but just for a few days." Barbie finally relented. "I've got to go to work Monday. C'mon, kids, let's go! Daddy will be mad when he gets home; we don't want that, do we?," rousing the kids up

"Do we have to?" said Darien. "I'm tired," rubbing his eyes sleepily. "Is Daddy mad at you?"

"No, what makes you say that?"

"I heard a lot of yelling."

"No we were just having a discussion," Barbie said, packing some of the kids' stuff.

"Are we going somewhere?"

"We'll be staying with Stacy for a few days."

"Why?"

"Because I said so. Now get a move on while I pack Bunny's stuff."

"Okay, we'll go in my car," said Stacy. She has a cobalt blue Corvette

"First let me pack a few things before we go."

"No need, you can borrow some of my stuff."

"Oh, no, he's back!" Barbie said worriedly.

"I know, let's go out that the back."

"Okay, hurry up."

Ken is turning the knob on the door when the girls ran out back hustling the kids out.

One thing for sure, Ken has never met any of Barbie's friends and vice versa. So it's highly unlikely that Ken knows what Stacy's car looks like.

"Hello, Babs? Kids?" Ken called to the empty house (well, with the exception of Doria). "I'm sorry I ran out on you like that. Let's make up."

After calling Barbie's name for awhile, Ken decides to talk to Doria to see if she knows where his wife went.

"Don't ask me, all I do here is work here. I don't get into anybody's business and nobody gets into mine" was the reply.

After Ken turns away, Doria smiles secretly, thinking, *Serves him right for treating her this way.*

With the kids away at sleep-away camp, Barbie & Stacy have a mini-slumber party. Ranger is crashing at a buddy of his.

"I haven't had this much fun since before I met Ken!"

"Remember, we're not supposed to mention him tonight."

"Yea, out with old, in with the new!" Barbie called out. "Let's go snag us some arm candy tomorrow night."

"But you're married and I'm with Ranger."

"You're right, Ken is a loser."

"Well we can go clubbing, dance the night away-have a girls' night out with the old crowd! It doesn't have to do with guys."

"Okay, okay, okay, enough wine. I think you're crazy drunk." Stacy said. '

As soon as Stacy takes the bottle away, Barbie is zoned out on the sofa. Quietly, she covers her with the shawl that is draped on the sofa, turning off the light as she left the room.

29

Connie Cyndi Chu

On Monday morning, she felt hungover still from Friday's night little slumber party. Sunday was a quiet day, acting like a third wheel on a date with Stacy and Ranger. They've popcorn and sodas, no alcohol, not even spiked soda. Boring!

She is prepared to work under her given name, Candice Hart. The first time she is called Candice she didn't acknowledge it until the person called her several times, then she remembers, *she* is Candice Hart!

She doesn't have a old cubicle like other employees; she has her own office being the Executive Assistant to CEO of Mattel John Jonero. She even have her own secretary. Cool, right? It gets better. She gets all-access pass to the CEO's limousine, his home, which is a mansion, of course that's cause she has to housesit from time to time. Whenever she housesits for him, she gets to use the amenities, which include a library, a full-size theatre with surround sound, an Olympic-sized pool that has a Jacuzzi and sauna. Not only that, there is a stable of purebred (of course) horses and ponies. There's also a tennis court. There's also a huge grand ballroom for dances. In the grand entrance of the mansion is a statue of the mythological Greek god Zeus, the mightiest of them all reeling a lightning bolt. The CEO welcomes her to invite friends over to have parties and such; she wouldn't need to clean up after a party-he has servants to do it. Oh yea, BTW did I mention the house has 7 rooms?! Lucky number 7!

Although CEO Jonero is unmarried, he is a playboy. He is a fine foxy fella. He is tall dark and handsome (J/k) No, really. He is muscular with a six-pack and is bronzed to nth degree. Not only that, he is tall and has the most aristocratic nose ever with the bluest-almost aqua-eyes ever.

The first time Barbie saw Jonero, she was burning with lust, but she kept her emotions in check (though she flirted innocently with him).

She started wearing makeup again. She stopped ever since she gotten married to that loser Ken.

"You've nice blue eyes," she purred flirtatiously, lowering her long eyelashes.

"Actually they're slate gray," Jonero said, looking her up and down. "Depending on the weather."

"You can have any color you want them to be," Barbie purred, putting her hand on his arm.

"Girl, you're *way* too young for me!"

Love in grand scheme of things is a mish-mash of trouble.

Connie Cyndi Chu

Barbie still stays at Stacy's house. Though Ken knows Stacy, he doesn't know where she lives, which is a good thing because she doesn't want to be around his temper anymore; she wants Jonero now. There's always rain on Barbie's parade-this time it's Ken, who still has her cell phone number, so what does he do? He keeps calling her and calling her ceaselessly, so what does *she* do? She changes her cell phone carrier from AT&T to Verizon. But before she does that, she texts Ken, "Im dvorcing u." Then she went to City Hall to file divorce papers, stating the reason as 'irreconcilable differences.' Within days, she hears back from the courthouse. The divorce papers went through-all it needs is a signature from Ken, her soon-to-be former spouse.

When the mail delivery service delivers the divorce papers, Ken apparently isn't home at the moment. However, when he gets home, he goes ballistic! *I'm ain't gonna sign this,* Ken thought. *I've got to get a lawyer to see if this is legit. Gotta get me a pro-bono lawyer."*

So he goes to the courthouse to seek out a pro-bono divorce lawyer. After his lawyer, R. Guttenberg, looks at the divorce papers, he said, "I'm afraid these divorce papers are legit. Your wife has served you with divorce papers. If you don't want to go to divorce court, just give her what she wants."

"Never!" Ken shouted. "I still love her! Listen, you get me to talk to her to see things my way.

"No can do," Guttenberg denied the request. "The divorce denies you contact with her."

"That whore!" shouted Ken. "She probably has a boyfriend on the side."

"So what have you decided?" Guttenberg asked.

"Go to divorce court!" yelled Ken. "Tell her I'll see her in court!"

Guttenberg told Barbie's lawyer-the best, most powerful lawyer in town-named Jane-Kate Jameson that they're going to divorce court. Since Barbie has one of Hollywood's most powerful, top-notch lawyers in all of Hollywood, Guttenberg and Ken didn't have a chance of prayer!

Ken refuses to withdraw from going into divorce court even after hearing that Barbie has a world-famous legal team behind her, introduced to her by Jonero. This legal team has helped many different kinds celebrities through civil and criminal cases.

On their first day of court, which is the first time they've seen each other since Barbie moved out of their Malibu condo and into Stacy's place.

"I love ya, Babs," Ken pleaded desperately.

"Well, you've got a funny way of showing it!" Barbie fumed angrily, turning away from him.

"Please don't go through with this. I'll do anything."

"Can you believe how pathetic he is?" Barbie whispered to one of her lawyers.

"Can you at least let me see the kids?" Ken continued as Barbie ignored him. "I'll bet Darien and Bun-Bun miss me."

At this, Barbie turned to Ken furiously, "I wouldn't let you see Darien and Bunny if you were their last living relative. I'm suing you for sole custody of the kids. I refuse to be your enabler, you got that?!"

"Well, we'll just see about that, won't we?" Ken said cockily.

When Barbie heard from her lawyers that they'll have to dig up everything on Ken, she was all for it, saying, "Why not? It's not like there's nothing I don't have anything to lose."

While Barbie's lawyers were busily working to find out about Ken's past. To worry about her kids and the divorce, Barbie herself continued her day job as Executive Assistant to the CEO of Mattel but was unable to flirt.

Several months later, her lawyers find out everything in Ken's past that she needs to know. Oh yeah, all the sordid details. Every last one. She finds all the 'ladies,' more like whores, he's been with. The list was longer than her arm!

"Are these the list of the girls who are friends with him or were intimate with him?" Barbie asked.

"Don't be so naïve, Barbie!" admonished Bailey, her private investigator who did the background check on Ken. "These girls are his friends, all right. More like friends with benefits."

"Omigod!" exclaimed Barbie. "These girls aren't ladies-these girls are whores! So he's been sleeping around with these whores?"

"It has been confirmed," said Bailey, nodding his head soberly.

"I'll drag his name through the mud! I'll slander him!"

"Okay, okay," Bailey said, putting his hand on her arm in order to appease Barbie. "Calm down."

"I can't calm down!" Barbie yelled, shaking his hand off her arm. "I'll ensure him that he'll never ever see the kids again! Oh no! What if-what if he gave me STIs? I gotta go get tested," said Barbie frantically. "But who'll watch the kids? Stacy isn't home yet." She looked at Bailey pleadingly.

"No, no way, I'm not watching your kids! I hate kids!" Bailey said hurriedly, practically running out the door. "Besides, I gotta go back to work!"

"Fine," said Barbie. "I'll just find someone else to look after the kids."

Connie Cyndi Chu

"Hey Stac," called Barbie as soon as she got a hold of her at her work, "I have to go out for a moment. Who would be a good sitter for the kids?"

"Why do you have to go out?"

After Barbie explained the situation, Stacy though it over, "There's Old Ms Groheimer, 2 doors down from me who baby-sits her grandkids when their parents are at work. Your kids can play with her grandkids."

Stacy would love to badmouth Ken, but ever the levelheaded young woman that she is, she remains firm, reasonable and sensible and a good friend to Barbie in her time of need.

Barbie places the kids in the care of Old Ms Groheimer, who turned out to be a trusty old woman with countless of grandkids because she has countless of kids herself. She also has 2 dogs, a beautiful tabby kitten.

Barbie goes to the free clinic. Upon learning that all tests and consultations are confidential and free, she was all for it. She did an all-out STIs test, testing to see if you have every single STI known to existence.

2 weeks later-

Barbie received a call from the free clinic to come down to get the results. Upon arrival, she heard that she needed more testing. But this time she needn't wait 2 weeks for results.

"Do you have kids?" the clinician asked.

"Yes," replied Barbie. "What of it?"

"Because you got gonorrhea," the clinician replied. "But it's perfectly curable." With that, the clinician turned away leaving Barbie all alone.

By the time, she has picked up the kids from Old Ms Groheimer and reached Stacy's place, tears are brimming in her eyes.

"Why are you crying, mommy?" asked Bunny her youngest

"Leave mom alone," Darien said. "She had a bad day."

"Go play, you guys," Barbie told them. "I'm gonna cook dinner while I wait for Stacy to come home."

When Stacy comes home, she listens like the good friend she is.

"But who are you gonna have kids with if you're divorcing him?"

"I might eventually have more kids in the future."

"You know, you could sue that jerk for emotional distress," suggested Stacy gently.

"No, I just want sole custody of the kids. I don't want to put the kids through that."

"Quit thinking about others, but what about *you?* What do you want?"

"I just want him out of my life, a nice fresh start, to have the past wipe clean."

"That's easier said than done, girl," said Stacy sympathetically, touching Barbie's arm gently with her hand.

The next day Barbie went to the courthouse to get a restraining order against her ex-husband, Ken to stay away from her and their kids, Bunny and Darien because she's afraid she might harm them although the only person he has harmed in the past was her. Ken has never laid a single hand on the kids, not even to molest them. But Barbie is afraid he might take out his anger on the kids and who knows what might happen then?

Since he had a pro-bono lawyer and she had a full professional team of lawyers, there is no doubt to everyone closest to them to who would win. Obviously, Barbie wins. But it isn't enough. She didn't want revenge. She just wants sole custody of the kids. Because of the wonderful legal team she has, she is granted immediate sole custody of the kids without dragging it through the court. They settle it out of court.

Although Barbie is granted sole custody of the kids, she wants to keep the restraining order intact against her ex-husband, Ken. She is fearful that Ken might come after her and the kids, so she decides to move without telling anyone. If she tells anyone, it'll get back to Ken, then he'll come after them and possibly kill 'em.

The only person she told was Stacy whom she trusts with her life.

Ken hasn't seen or heard from Barbie in days and even weeks. Not unusual since there is a restraining order against him to stay away from Barbie. And Ken knew Stacy knew where Barbie is. Stacy wouldn't say even though Ken cajoles her, acts aggressive towards her and obnoxious towards her. For days, he would harass Stacy till there is no end.

At the end, he threatened, "I'm gonna tear you from limb to limb if you don't tell me where she is. I know you know where she is."

To Stacy, mum's the word if she wants to keep Barbie safe from the low-lifes of Ken Dall.

He left as quickly as he came. As soon as he leaves, however, Stacy quickly calls Tulsa, where Barbie moved to. She always wanted to live in the countryside.

39

Connie Cyndi Chu

Brring brring brring! The sound of the phone is echo-y in the small ranch villa since Barbie was working online at home while her kiddies are at school. Of course, they have to go the free local public school.

"Babs' Office & Retail," answered Barbie chirpily. Even though Ken called her Babs, the nickname didn't invoked any bad memories. As a child, her parents called her Babs and occasionally her closest pals did too. Her platinum blonde locks changed back to its original color: red. Yep, guys n' dolls, Barbie was originally once a redhead.

"Hi baby," whispered Stacy. "How are doin'?"

"Why are we whispering?" Barbie said softly.

"Because he's outside, watching, waiting for my next move. He's stalking me. Why, oh, why did you leave me with him? He knows I know where you are."

"Just stand your ground," said Barbie quietly and thoughtfully. "Don't let him push you around. Look, the kiddies are back. I'll talk to you later. 'Bye"

Barbie is trying to remove everything from her old life. Including her bestie, Stacy.

"Wanna go get some ice cream, kids?!"

"What are you up to, Mom?" asked Darien suspiciously

"We're going into town to change my phone for a brand-new one. Will that be fun?!"

"But how'll Stacy contact us in case of an emergency?"

"Forget her, will you, kid?" said Barbie in annoyance. "I just want you kids to have a whole brand-new life, is all."

"Okay, I agreed, Mom," Darien said. "We should have new start cos we're living in a new town, and we're"-pulling his sister closer-"makin' new friends. I don't see why you shouldn't either."

"Thanks for understanding, guys!" Barbie said, hugging all of his eight-year-old self to her. "Maybe you should get a phone also."

After Barbie got a new phone with a different phone number, she really did gave Darien, being the oldest and all, a cell phone of his own.

~The End~

Ranger-Stacy Barbie-Ken

/

Darien 8, Bunny 6
Future Defined! Reaching for Beyond the Limits!

Connie Cyndi Chu

It is the year 3000. People, if that's what you called them, are half humans/half aliens. They have space colonies on other planets because earth is overrun by androids. They live in space pods, which are like huge, fortress-like Tupperware, which keeps the species youthful and vibrant. This prevents people, er, species from aging. They don't eat; they absorb energy in their Tupperware homes. They have space cars, which are computer-operated-they don't need gasoline or electricity. They just put in the destination in the computer in the space car, and they are at their destination in a matter of seconds. They can travel to other planets by space cars.

The latest craze is cryogenically frozen species or rather, humans. A millennium ago, it was being developed. Now it is the rage. The first cryogenically frozen woman is discovered in an abandoned laboratory by an android on earth. After the discovery, the cryogenically wonder is sent off to a brightly-lit laboratory, all sterilized with everything in stainless steel to Venus. The inhabitants, as are practically on every single planet, is habited by half-humans/half-aliens or huliens. They called it a most 'curious find.' When they opened it up, they asked, "Who are you? *What* are you?" They've never seen a real complete human species before. Up till now, aliens and humans species merge together with no thought whatsoever forming half aliens-half humans or if you will, huliens. Half aliens-half humans have been past down throughout the generations since man realized that aliens are just as intelligent as the next homo sapiens excluding androids. Even though they speak alien-speak, they also are fluent in English.

"W-w-who are you?" Janie asked. "What is this place?"

"We are Venusans," one of the half aliens-half humans answered. "You are on the planet Venus." This species has huge, bulging eyes. He has an antennae, crinkled face like a pit bull. He also has huge, pointy Spock-like ears. His fingers are pointy and scraggly.. His skin is wrinkly even though he is young. When he speaks, his voice is rough; it has an edge to it.

"Am I dreaming?" Janie wondered aloud. "Nobody has even *explored* Venus yet."

"A lot of people have already inhabited the other planets."

"What about earth?"

"What *about* earth? That planet is overrun by androids."

"Now, would you mind telling me who and what you are?"

;"One more thing: I was wondering what year is it?"

The ringleader of the half aliens-half humans looked at the others, bewildered. They converse in their alien tongue for a while, "Just humor her."

"Okay," the head of the group said, "It is the year 3000."

"What *language* were you speaking?"

"Alien-speak," said the ringleader. "Any more questions?"

"Oh my God," Janie said, astonished. "It is the year 3000! Can I get a mirror?"

"As you wish, darling," said the ringleader, leading her to a full-length mirror. "By the way, my name's Isadore. What's yours?"

"My name is Jane. Friends called me Janie. Can I ask you one more question?"

"Go ahead."

"What are you?"

:"We're huliens-a half human-half alien species. We've been wondering the same thing about you."

"Oh, me? I'm a human."

43

Connie Cyndi Chu

:"Here you are, Janie. Here's a mirror." Isadore took her to a full-length mirror in the hallway.

When she went into the cryogenically-frozen chamber, she weighed nearly 1000 pounds give or take. Her skin and hair was dull. Now, looking at the mirror, she look so svelte and her skin, not to mention her hair, was positively glowing.

"Oh my God, look how wonderful I look!" Janie is surprised by the image looking back at her. She can't help saying, "The years had been good to me-I went from being an ugly duckling to a beautiful swan!" Janie kept admiring herself in the mirror. "Not to be vain or anything, but I look *good*," turning every which way till she notices the hulien looking oddly at her.

"Don't you huliens care about body image?"

"No, we don't," Isadore replied.

"Huh." Janie said, turning away from the mirror.

Now, turning to Isadore, she asked, "Do I have any living relatives or even some friends left?"

Isadore replied, "You'll have to go to the local geneticist to find out if you have any blood relatives left. I'll give you the address."

After Isadore gives her the address, he says, "You'll have to hail a space cab. I'll help you since it's your first time here."

When Janie got to the geneticist, she finds out that all hope is *not* lost. After filling out the necessary documents via computer, she is in! She finds out she has one living relative, Elizabeth Jane 'Lizzie Janie;' friends and close acquaintances call her LJ, who lives on planet Mars, a hulien. She is Janie's great-great-great-granddaughter. (She was cryogenically frozen the day of her wedding. She had a baby before she got married. She wanted to get married because she had a baby.)

Planet Angel Dee-lite!

So Janie hops on the next upcoming space cab, and off she goes! It did not even take her an hour; it takes her less than that to reach Mars. The cabdriver consults his GPS navigation system in his cab, and within minutes they're there! (See how advanced technology is-now you have no possible way of getting lost!)

Janie gets out of the space cab to pay the cabdriver, "Already taken care of, miss."

"Oh, thanks."

"Certainly, my dear," said the friendly cabdriver. "Hope you find what you're looking for. Good luck!"

"Thanks, sir."

Janie finally looks up at where the cab drops her off at: it is a huge-I mean *huge*-mansion. *Gee*, she thought, *my relative must be rich!*

When she buzzes the intercom, a young-ish female voice answered, "What is your business?"

"I would like to see L J. I'm her great-great-great-grandmother."

Silence, then: "Impossible! My great-great-great-grandmother Janie disappeared, never to be found again, so family legend has it. *This* I've got to see for myself!

L J has human features, but quite a few things are different about her. First off, she has pointy, Spock-like ears and antennae, all the better to send messages across the galaxy. And that's about it. L J's skin and hair is positively radiant, and is as slim as a palm tree.

"You're Janie, my great-great-great-grandmother?" L J said incredulously upon meeting her face-to-face for the first time.

"Yep," replied Janie, perturbed. "And you are L J? But you can't be L J. You're not even human!"

45

Connie Cyndi Chu

"I am part human and part alien, and I am L J, your great-great-great-granddaughter," replied L J. "And just what are you? I mean, aside from being my great-great-great-grandmother?"

"I'm a human being," Janie replied sadly. "The last of its kind, as I've been told."

"No way!" L J exclaimed. "You're the last of your kind? I don't believe it! I really don't! There must be some humans *somewhere* in this universe."

"So what *happened* to you?" L J continued. Family legend has it that you disappeared off the face of the earth, never to be found again, much like Amelia Earhart or something like that…"

"I disappeared, all right," Janie agreed. "I was cryogenically frozen as part of an experiment. My family was against it. I didn't tell anyone and I mean *no one* about my whereabouts. That's why no one knew where I was."

"Okay, I believe you," L J said. "Come in, come in. Won't you please sit down?"

Upon entering the foyer, L J leads Janie to the parlor. She can't help but look as she passes by each room. Everything is sterling silver as though everything needs to be sterilized. It is sterilized because the human race started dying off in 2050 because everything started to have germs so that's why now everyone needs to live in a germ-free environment or perish, just *positively* perish! That is also why humans and aliens have merged together, forming the new species: huliens. It looks like a science laboratory, but, in reality, it is Lizzie Janie's home. They finally reach the sitting room, but from Janie's viewpoint, there isn't anywhere to sit until Lizzie Janie shows her where to sit: on pods. People sit on pods, where it's all sealed up although there are holes to talk right through.

"So what's the year 3000 like?" Janie asked when they finally settle down. "For example, do you have an entertainment center?"

"Oh, do we!" L J exclaimed. "We built this house from the ground up, and we made one specific room most specially for our entertainment center. Wanna check it out?"

"Sure thing!" replied Janie, falling into Lizzie Janie's steps. "Can you hook it up to all throughout the galaxy?"

LJ replied with Janie close behind, "Sure, if you want."

They enter one of the most largest rooms in the house. This room, too, is made out of sterling silver. But the entertainment is, to Janie, mind-blowing! I mean, every single surface is covered with one or another kind of entertainment hardware. Some are laid out in disuse; others are just plain out-of-date but still in mint condition.

Upon entering the entertainment center, it brought tears to Janie's eyes. She starts to feel nostalgic for her family that she left back in the 21st century. She had a wild brother who loved-just positively *loved*-hi-tech gadgets who passed the love onto her, his only sister. As kids, they were a team-she was the Bonnie and he was the Clyde. He was older than her by two years. They were inseparable until the day he left for college, got married and have kids. (Yes, in that order.)

Her parents were often proud of her brother rather than of her. She decided she better made her own path in life, so she did all these experiments. One of these crazy, off-the-wall experiments was that she got cryogenically frozen. Being cryogenically frozen was a work-in-progress back in the 21st century, but she went for it anyways. Her parents disapproved of her experiments, so she told no one, including her best friend, her brother, because she knew it would get back to her parents

Connie Cyndi Chu

because her brother was more close to her parents than her. After her brother moved out, she tried all these crazy, cockamamie schemes.

Now she is starting over, trying out all these experiments yet again because she wants to find a way to either go back in time when she was first cryogenically frozen or to discover a way to make human contact with an actual human. Instead of being tested, she will be the one concocting the experiments this time around. She's taking crazy chances. She's always been a risk-taker, bending the rules when she didn't agreed to them. Her brother, however, was just the opposite.

As she reminisces, she feels saddened that she no longer has her brother to share this with and runs out of the room, nearly crashing headlong into Lizzie Janie's husband, a hulien who looks like a human except for his tentacles and pointy ears.

"Oh, I'm sorry!" Janie exclaimed. "What-you're *another* half human-half alien?! Is there *any* humans left?!"

"Better go after her," L J's husband said. "She seems upset."

Janie runs out of the room, with L J close at her heels.

"I know you're upset, but the world is full of huliens-half humans/half aliens; plus earth is overrun by androids," L J told Janie gently.

Janie cries, "What I crave is human contact, not your 'huliens' or whatever you called yourself now. And I can't communicate with androids-you control 'em." Janie covers her tear-stained face with her hands, running out of the huge Tupperware-like mansion. .

L J thinks for a moment. "I think I know of a place where there's only humans around. Some of our huliens gave birth to human babies, but we sent them to the orphanage."

"That's terrible," Janie commiserated. "But I'm thinking about humans that I can relate to, not babies."

"See ya," Janie said tearfully.

"'Bye!" L J said cheerfully. "Cheer up!"

Janie hails the first space cab she sees to go back to Venus, where she first starts off.

She is, to be frank, in a state of shock. She keeps saying in a monotone over and over again, "I can't be the last living human alive." She is in a state of shock for maybe 24 hours, then she falls into a state of depression. She crashes in with one of the huliens in their Tupperware houses. The hulien finds her, not the other way around. It just so happens to be the 'ringleader' of the huliens, Isadore although there's no such thing as leadership; everyone is independent, on their own; it is *not* a police state, thank god! Janie thinks the huliens have a 'ringleader' because that's how her kind works.

Isadore knows that Janie is in a state of depression. He didn't know what would cheer her up. He finds out from her that she is depressed because there's a lack of human contact in the universe, as of now. So he gets her a feline-android to keep her company. Originally named 3PX-579, she renames it Kitty-Kat or Kits for short. It gives her the motivation to work harder than ever before.

She decides she better get started on doing experiments on making human contact. All those experiments she did a millennium ago sort of are engrained into her brain. And with a college degree in biotechnology to back it up, she decides to setup her own laboratory; in the past, she has always done her own experiments with help from only her faithful assistant, Jananne. But now sadly, even her faithful assistant is gone too, so she has her faithful companion feline android, Kits, to make up for it although it is no comparison to the real deal.

49

Connie Cyndi Chu

She decides to make human and some sort of animal contact by using satellites with the sounds of practically anything-I mean *anything*. She sets up three huge-I mean *huge*-satellite dishes, facing them toward the universe, which connects to a radar screen to see where the sounds are coming from. She comes up with a device that tells the difference between android, half humans-half aliens or rather, huliens and real live humans and animals, if those still exist. Wherever there are humans, there are bound to be animals.

After a few backfires, she finally surprisingly comes up with a human signal. It comes from an underworld of humans called the Untouchables who *haven't* merged with aliens. This planet, Spaceverse, which is a billion light years, maybe eons and eons, away, is unreachable.

She didn't see any reason to go to the trouble of reaching out to them. I mean, why bother? Although she gives up hope of uniting with her kind, she remains in contact with them through teleportation traveling back and forth through the space-time continuum. Both Janie and the Untouchables are jubilant to find someone of their kind still cohabiting this universe in this day and age

But teleportation isn't enough; it didn't satisfy her need for actual human contact for Janie and animal contact for Kits. She and Kits wanted to have actual human contact and to see actual animals. So she decides to create her very own space pod that could surpass light years beyond light years in a matter of seconds. When you're on it, you feel like you're traveling through time not through the space-time continuum, which in fact, is what you're doing.

After a billion and one (that's an exaggeration!) almost successes and failures, she actually pulls it off! With a pull of the trigger, Janie and Kits are off! Whoosh! She travels through the time-space continuum in a matter of seconds! The minute she gets off the ship, she is greeted by one human, and then another.

Most of them have pets; some don't. They even see a kitten, Fluffy; her owner is a lady named Rachel-Ann. Both Janie and Kits get along famously with Fluffy and Rachel-Ann.

Janie is so happy to be amongst humans once again that she didn't even care if Kits is a feline-android. Oh, to be surrounded by humans once again! She feels overwhelmed with happiness! Oh, there is much rejoicing going on! There is singing and dancing! Hooray! Happy days are here again! Oh, yeah, boy! She rejoices with the other humans. She no longer thinks deathly thoughts because now she has something to live for. She felt depressed when she discovered that there's no human life in the universe; but her experiments haven't yet failed her yet. Rejoice! Rejoice! Hallelujah! They won't ever go back to the place filled with huliens because they finally find what they are looking for: true human and animal contact!

Moral: Dreams are possible, you just have to have the motivation to attain them. Everything's-and I mean *everything* is within our reach!

Connie Cyndi Chu
Girls (Absolutely, Positively Without a Doubt) Rule!!!

There's no one- Absolutely No one- you can depend on except for us girls.
NO BOYS ALLOWED!

Here's a lil Mother Goose rhyme that says it all
What are little boys made of?
Snips and snails, and puppy dogs tails
That's what little boys are made of!"
What are little girls made of?
"Sugar and spice and all things nice
That's what little girls are made of!"

"O no! Have u heard?!? Jan said.

"What?" her sister, Amy said. "What happened, Jan?"

"There was a meteorite shower last night, right?" Jan explained. "All and the male race was wiped out."

"OMG!" said Amy. "What about Bobby?" Bobby was her estranged husband.

"All gone," said Jan sadly But inwardly she was happy, doing somersaults insides because she despised all and any men she came across.

Jan and Amy are both identical twins sisters with 2 minutes apart. Although Jan is the younger old twin and Amy the older one, sometimes she felt like the older twin due to her sage and wise advice. They got brown hair and had heterochromia, which meant they had different color eyes. They've lesbian parents, whose mother Lara got pregnant with them through one of her open relationships, which were still going on, but they've moved into a commune. Bobby and Amy had adorable identical six-year-old twin girls, Carla and Darla, who were away at an all-girls boarding school, Sweetcuffs Boarding School for Girls, which was run by women only- their motto was simply: Girls Rule; they've been there since pre-k. They were blond but also were hererochromia.

Jan despised all and any men because Amy had been having a lot of difficulty with men, and Amy always went to Jan to solace in the form of turning to the bottle-Amy was an alcoholic-or a shoulder to cry on when she couldn't take it anymore or even when she felt drastic a couple months she attempted suicide. Jan thought Bobby was the scum of the earth for leaving poor Amy cause even when they were kids Amy was always clingy-she tended to lack self-esteem.

Jan herself was an accomplished career women, having open her own business in shoe design and was about to open a new café. Her short-term plan was to become her own boss. Next step was to have her own business. Thirdly, she wanted to expand it to a franchise.

Having designed shoes for all the major shoe companies and making a huge profit at it, she decided to aim higher-she wanted to design a specific shoe for multi-purposes like running, walking, etcera for women. Having designed the shoes and then having rejected by all the major shoe companies that are mostly run by men, she decided to form her own shoe company. She always did have this free-spirit attitude about her, and no one can denied her that.

Anyway when she heard the news that men were depleted from the planet, outwardly she was sad but inwardly she was jubilant.

"Amy, Sweet Amy," Jan whispered, hugging her close. "Are you alright?"

"No, I'm not." Amy replied. "I've got to call my girls. See if they're alright," hurrying off while drying her tears quickly on sleeve.

Connie Cyndi Chu

Amy ran off to a quiet place to make a call to her darlings. Darla and Carla, her prides of her joy, were sheltered since babyhood, so they didn't know about the catastrophe that lay ahead.

Said Amy to Carla, the eldest twin by 30 seconds; she sometimes seemed older than her six years, "Life will never be the same again."

"What do you mean, mommy?" Carla asked worriedly.

"Just close to your sister-at all times."

"But you got me so worried, mommy," Carla cried. "Whatsamatter?"

"Okay, if I tell you, will you promise not to tell your sister. You know your sister won't be able to handle it."

"Okay, okay," said Carla. "Now will you tell me?"

"The world, as we know it, has been depleted of mankind. There is no more male race from this moment on."

"You gotta be kidding me!" said Carla both astonished and shocked.

"Yes, sweetheart, it is, without a doubt, the truth."

"How'll I be able to keep this secret from Darla? Carla agonized. "She's been seeing this young man, Erik who is twelve. She thought Erik had stood her up."

"Okay, if you must tell her, break it to her as gently as you could" Amy finally consented.

"What about Daddy?" Carla asked. "Is he alright?"

"No I'm afraid he's not," said Amy disappointedly. "He's one of the many male casualties"

"Oh no!" Carla screamed into the phone. "Darla! Darla! Come quick! Daddy's dead!"

"I'm back, Mom," said Carla, sobbing. "What do you want us girls to do?" Both girls were close to their father, but Darla was the tomboy of the two-the son their father never had

"Just stay where you are - you girls are safe where you are," said Amy morosely.

While Amy was talking to her daughters, Jan was celebrating the coming of a new age. She brought the champagne out and was drinking to 'love, joy and queendom of that is sweet! No more rotten boys to rot away at our core! Oh yeh this is the day to celebrate! Probably was struck down by the meteorite because they were killing each other through war, no more guys to beat us when we're down, no more violence at the hands of those male chauvinistic pigs. Slimeballs! They deserve to die!"

At the moment her twin came back and heard the end of Jan's monologue. "THEY DESERVE TO DIE. HOW COULD YOU SAY SUCH A THING!?!" she screamed in tears.

"But you always have told boys gave you such grief," Jan pointed out.

"It doesn't mean I want them to die," Amy cried.

"Okay, okay," Jan relented. "You've always been boy-crazy, even when we were teens."

"Boys may be a total turn-off for you, but I love my boys."

"Wanna have a drink, sis?"

"Yes, please," Amy replied. "How about vodka with OJ on the side? Thanks so much, baby." She drank whenever there was pain involved to avoid dealing with emotional distress. In this case, she was stressing over losing guys.

Meanwhile Amy's darling twins decided to come home due to the loss of twins' father and Darla's boyfriend Erik since they can't even concentrate on their schoolwork. Actually, Sweetcuffs closed down temporarily because none of the girls could even concentrate because their fathers or male relatives had died in the meteorite shower.

55

Connie Cyndi Chu

Even though Amy's twins were only six years old, they were able to take the train by themselves. They were arrived just as their aunt Jan was about to carry their sleeping mother upstairs. They saw the empty bottle of vodka and empty carton of orange juice, which so happens to be their mother's favorite combination.

"Hush!" whispered Jan, carrying Amy upstairs. "Be right back. I'll deal with you two in a moment."

Jan carried her sister up the creaking stairs, cradling her in her arms. Amy's long hair was falling nearly touching the carpet.

When Jan reached Amy's room, she placed her gently on her bed, brushing her damp hair back and kissing her forehead. "Amy, my dear girl," Jan whispered oh-so-softly, "we're better off without boys in our lives," turning on the night light and leaving the door ajar, just the way she always had liked it (even she had kids of her own).

As Jan came down the stairs, missing the creaking stairs this time around, she called out to her sister's twins. "Carla, Darla!"

"Hi Auntie Jan," called Carla and Darla.

"Why are you girls home?" Jan asked.

Carla replied, "School's closed. What happened to Mom?"

"She's just tired, had a long day, and needs a nap."

"Did you do something to her?" Carla, the smarter one and the one who got right to the point, asked. "Is she drunk? "No, she's not drunk," said Jan dismissively. "She's my sister. Why you little girls asked such questions? You don't know anything about anything."

"Are you calling us stupid?" Darla finally spoke up.

"No, stop putting words in my mouth," said Jan

"We see empty vodka and orange bottles lying around," Carla insisted. "That's Mom's favorite combo."

"Okay, I give," Jan said. "So I did get your mom good and drunk. That's cause she was making a great fuss about the meteorite shower."

"That killed all of the male species," said Darla. "Including our father and my boyfriend."

"I wouldn't be surprised, Auntie Jan," said Carla, "if you wish all of the men to be killed off."

"Me?" Jan said innocently. "I didn't do anything." As a matter of fact, she prayed for something to happen to the men of this world the night before. And lo and behold, something incredible did happen.

"It is a known fact that you hate men, Auntie Jan," said Darla. "You hate men so much, you're a lesbian. You probably wish every living male species would be killed off, become endangered and whatnot."

"Alright, guys, I mean, girls, let's make good of a bad situation," Carla intervened. "Let's not make do of what we got."

"But how can we survive without men, boys, whatever?" Darla asked

"The way we always had," Jan said. "We never need oversexed, sex-crazed, sports fanatics high-testosterone creeps in our lives, do we now?"

"No I guess not," Darla said.

"They are the ones who cause this planet to be overpopulated, not us womenfolk. 'Cause they enjoyed getting laid, not us. Our main goal is just to satisfy them."

"Whatevs, Auntie Jan," said Darla dismissively.

"Alrighty, girls," Carla said. "Let's just call a truce."

"Okay, okay," Darla said, "truce, shaking on it."

"Let's agree to disagree, okay?" asked Jan, shaking her niece's hand.

"Okay," said Darla.

Connie Cyndi Chu

After agreeing to disagree and do more work teamwork and less fighting, they broke up into groups of four. True, there were only 3 people since Jan can't even trust her own sister because of her drinking problem. But Jan had some connections being a top-notch criminal pro-bono lawyer for the defenseless. She contacted her go-to girl, Ira, who's also her best friend and her paralegal and assistant to many of the politicos in their town of Honeycomb Beach, including the DA, Lana Osby

"Hey girlfriend," said Jan upon reaching her

"Excuse me?" asked Ira. "Who is this?"

"This is your bestie, Jan," Jan replied.

"Oh, it's you, no time to chat now," said a flustered Ira "We've a crisis; everything's chaotic here!"

"That's why I was calling," said Jan. "I want to make things easier for you."

"I'm listenin'," said Ira, taking 3 gulps of Vitaminwater.

"There are no more male species, right?" said Jan. "What I'm thinkin' is, we should get 4 girls and divide them up, North, South, East and West and have 'em patrol the world. Got it?"

"Got it! But what about my duties as an assistant to the DA?"

"Leave it," said Jan firmly. "We've got more important things to worry about."

"Okey dokey," said Ira, "just lemme get my girls ready and I'm off."

"Your girls?" said Jan. "You mean your entourage?"

"Yeah, that," said Ira. "With that big task, I can't go about it alone."

"I see what you mean," agreed Jan. "I guess you're right. We divide into teams of 4 to go to North, South, East & West, okay? Sounds like a better plan?"

"Much," said Ira. "Okay, break!"

"Let's synchronize our watches when we'll next meet."

"Okay, let's do it!"

After Jan told the twins the plan, they decided to get their friends together to form a group to survey the areas they've been assigned to watch over. The twins and their friends were to watch the Northern and Southern parts of the world while Jan and Ira and their friends were to patrol the Western and Eastern parts of the world.

After they synchronize their watches, they set off with their entourages to their assigned destinations. The twins went off separately for the first time evah. Carla and friends went off to the Northern part of the world while Darla and her groupies went off to the Southern part of the world. Ira and her friends decided they want to go to the Western part of the world while Jan and her friends had no choice but to choose the Eastern having all parts of the world already being chosen

At first, the twins were sad to leave each other but knew they would see each other very soon. They gave each other a long bear hug. Carla said, "Be careful out there, honey. Luv ya."

"With all my hart," said Darla.

"What'll we do about Mom?"

"Just leave her here," replied Jan. "She'll be alright for a few hours. I already locked the liquor cabinet, so there's no problem. Ready, girls?"

"Ready!" they chorused.

The devastation was ginormous; everything was in total and complete chaos. All of womankind was stunned, stupefied. They can't believe it. Jan and friends were in the Eastern part of the world and the devastation was terrible. Although it was a 3rd world country, the people were mourning over their dead male relatives, whom they depended on for their livelihood. They women may be fieldhands, but the men provided the moolah. They did the heavy-duty work like chop wood, sell meat, etc, but without the men in their lives, how would they be able to survive?

Connie Cyndi Chu

In the Western part of the world, hearts were breakin' everywhere. Even people with alternative lifestyles. They were mourning over male relatives, male companions, and male friends. Nobody was celebrating, not even those loathsome man-haters. They acted like the world was ending, for Pete's sake. They just dropped dead in their tracks and cried as if the world had just ended. And in a way, the world had just ended. Even on the street women were bawling their eyes out. They didn't care who saw them because everybody was crying anyways.

In the Southern part of the world, Darla's area, where people were scant, there was not much to see but polar bears lookin' for the young'uns aimlessly. Also, there were no men out to hunt and gather food in the jungle anymore, so the women have to fend for themselves with what they already had.

In the Northern part of the world, there was no more Santy Claus, only Mrs. Claus and what's remaining of her female elves. So there's no more Christmas. Also, they're no more Eskimos men, Eskimo women. The Eskimo men did the hunting and gathering. Without men, the Eskimo women won't be able to survive. Also, there's no more Northern lights cos that was controlled by men.

When Carla and Darla and Jan and Ira rendezvoused at Jan's place at the synchronized time, they reported that women were weak and needed male companionship.

"This is not so!" Jan said. "We could so do without male companionship. We need to send out a public service announcement that we can rise up without men; we do it without 'em!"

"Yes!" the teen twins raised their fists high in the air together. "You go Auntie Jan!"

"Yes," said Ira, "but you're all talk and no action. We can send out a public broadcast announcement, but who would listen? Everybody everywhere is mourning for their lost one."

"We can at least tried," said Jan.

"I guess trying never hurt anyone," said Ira reluctantly.

"Remember our school's motto: Girls Rule?" Carla asked.

"Yeah," said Darla slowly "What about it?"

"My poor misguided sister," said Carla sympathetically. "Well, now that all of male species are gone," continued Carla, "we can put it into practice by showing those clingy girls that girls can do stuff even better than guys. 1000 folds better even!"

"Yeah," roared Darla. "That's the ticket! We girls rock!"

The teen twins and Jan and Ira sent out the PSA, via the WWW and doing old-school advertisements in all forms of media which included print, which included bulletin boards, magazines, bus stations & subways. Pretty soon all the advertisements were filled with the PSA. And the PSA on the WWW had gone viral. It said the following:

Girlz! Girlz! Girlz! Girlz! Girlz!

Listen up, ladies!

You are not weak, fragile, clingy creatures-

You can do without men

Men just want us to satisfy their sexual urges!

Let's be stronger that-

We can carry on without our male subordinates!

We are mighty than those L-O-S-E-R-S!

61

Connie Cyndi Chu

We need to regain our own respect for ourselves-

not depend on some Neanderthals!

This is <u>not</u> an X--rated advertisement

Girlz! Girlz! Girlz! Girlz! Girlz!

When all the women in the world got wind of this message, grrl did they realized the people- Carla and Darla and Ira and Jan- were right, so they decided to do something about it. First off, the ladies of the world decided it wasn't worth it to mourn over the loss of the male friends. Men, they thought, are just a buncha freeloaders and emotional excess baggage.
They could do things 1000 times better than men-those scumbags-could and they did. In the East, the women following in the footsteps of the menfolk learned how to chop wood, sell meat. At first, it was oh-so-hard, then they got they got the hang off it.
Everyday is a work-in-progress.

Over in the West, that's right, men are worthless, who needed them anyway? We can do things way better than 'em any old day. It is called self-reliance. We don't need any men to help us out. They never helped us when we asked 'em to anyways. They're really pathetic. What am I doing crying over 'em anyways? I'm wasting my time crying over spilt milk. We can do things without worrying about consulting our guys. We can always have girls' night our. Life is lookin' up.
In the Northern and Southern parts of the world, the ladies went hunting. They knew how to do it cos they saw their men done it a million times before. Monkey do monkey see. Watching seemed easy, but actually doing it? Not so much. In the beginning, it was so hard. Since

all the animals were all of the female species, it was much easier to catch. All you have to do was get the said animal away from its babies. If you got the babies first, then the mama animal will be furious.

The women hunters didn't realize this till the end when they attacked the unguarded babies because it was easier, but the mama animal sensing danger hurrying back as quick as lightning. The women hunters, who were scared out of their wits, decided to try another day. Next day, they tried again, only this time, they decided to aim their weapons, which were inherited from their male friends, at the mama animal. They decided to sneak up behind the mama animal

The headhunter, a woman named Carlita who had gone hunting with her husband, knew that you should attack the mama animal first. She also knew how to use a rifle.

"Quiet now, ladies," Carlita whispered.

But one of them accidentally stepped on a twig. CRACK!

"Hush!" Carlita tried to hush the other ladies

But it was too late. The mama animal turned with a low growl.

"C'mon, somebody, shoot 'er" screamed Carlita, "before she gets us!"

All the women were panicking, running in every which way; only Carlita was left behind. There was no choice; it was up to her to shoot the mama animal. With nobody left but her to defend the mama animal-showing girls were a buncha wimps-she shot the mama animal right between the eyes, not knowing what hit her. After she shot the mama animal, she took the carcass, leaving behind the babies whining for their mother.

Back at camp, she called her so-called friends out. "You guys are a buncha wussies. You left me standing out there alone. You're my back up. Where were you guys when I needed you?"

"Looks to me you got the animal without our help." Johanna pointed out.

Connie Cyndi Chu

"Yeah," Carlita said. "But I could've gotten help with the babies. We could've used the babies to make clothes or something."

Up in the North Pole, there was now no more Santy Claus. But there were all those female elves and Mrs. Claus. Mrs. Claus oversaw the running of the kitchen. Usually, the female elves baked Christmas cookies and other Christmas goodies, which included fruitcakes of all kinds. Delectable! (That's how Santa Claus was so heavy-set because he ate a lot of goodies all throughout the year!) The male elves usually made the presents for all those good girls and gave a bag of coal to the naughty ones while Santa Claus checked off whose been naughty or nice. (How does he do it? Is he like God or something?)

Now that there's no more Santa Clause, Mrs. Claus must take over the duties that used to be used Santa Claus'. Not only must she coordinate the kitchen that baked the Christmas cookies and other Christmas goodies, she must also run the elves workshop that used to be run by male elves but now needed to be run by female elves. She gotta checked whose been naughty or nice; if they've been nice they've received their heart's desires. On the other hand, if they've been naughty, they've only received a bag of coal. They've no choice, otherwise there would be NO MORE CHRISTMAS! And we can't have that, can we, now? Also, in order to replace Santy Claus on the sleigh, with the 7 reindeers herding them forward, she must deliver the presents to the good little girls (since there's no more Santa Claus, imposter or the real deal) since Santy Claus was male and all male species were wiped off the face of the earth.

The female ruler of world came about when the whole world voted for youngest teenage girls in the world, which so happened to be Carla and Darla. Since Carla clearly was the smarter one, and Darla the ditzy, perky one, Carla became the female ruler of the world with Darla being Carla's sidekick.

The female ruler of the world abolished all prisons and replaced by reformatories and rehabilitation centers, where women can change their lives for the better. The female ruler turned all prisons into rehabs or reformatory. Prisms may be a waste of taxpayers' money.

but reformatories and rehabilitation centers are court-appointed. If women broke the law, they have to go to reformatory. Or if they do drugs or cited for DUI, they must go to rehab. If girls up to adult age, that would be 18 years of age, committed a crime, they would be sent to a reformatory for crimes other than doing drugs or underage drinking. But there are also adult reformatories, where women learn a trade or a skill free of charge-otherwise known as community college. But in this case, instructors from a community college were brought into teach these women.

Population was controlled because no sex-crazed, testosterone-filled boy wanna boned up with some silly boy-crazy, two-timing, backstabbing girl. Before the meteorite shower, whenever boys made out with girls, and one thing led to another, they almost always ended up in each other's beds. 9 out of 10 girls at the local high school from the upperclass were pregnant or have babies (8 out of 10 girls from the lower class have babies or pregnant), but the fathers were too irresponsible to own up to their mistakes. The parents have to kick 'em out or they have to take care of the babies on their own.

After the meteorite shower, however, there were no more boys, so no more hot, horny foreplay from the guys. To the girls who were already pregnant or already have babies, well, they'll just have to deal. I mean, they never have the support of the baby daddy in the first place. They could handle it. They are made of tougher stuff than this. They don't and won't lead on any man for help. They won't break now. They gotta show a whole new generation of women that they can stand on their own two feet without relying on men to bailing 'em out. They're no damsels in distress, like 'Woe is me.' No siree. They'll stand tall. They'll survive-they're survivors. I mean, who gave birth to 'em? Us women did. We were in labor a million hours; ok that's an exaggeration, maybe half a day.

Connie Cyndi Chu
Goddesses and Superheroes Unite!

I am Desireé, goddess of desire from the planet Zortec. I have many powers, among them I can be a shapeshifter. That is I can take on any form you please. I have taken on so many forms I have forgotten my true form.

Like all gods and goddesses from planet Zortec, I have 9 lives like cats that are our planet's guardians. Each time I am reborn I take another goddess die and another goddess is born like phoenix rising from the dead. Right now, I'm onto my 2nd life. But some of that anger is still at the surface, ready to boil over any minute. Anything can tip the scales. I am goddess of desire, As Desireé, I have the widest, so huge it practically takes up my whole face, bluest eyes of the galaxy, an aristocratic nose, flaxen hair and flawless skin as if it's craved from marble. We are immune from any and all diseases except meteorite showers. A meteorite shower obliterated all of the known gods in the planet Zortec.

In planet Zortec, the Mighty Goddess of all that she rules- Goddess of Desire's mother Goddess of Faith, whose name is what she stands for. On earth, little girls learn how to drive. But at age 16, on the planet Zortec, all little girls must seek their soulmates. They are given two years to find a soulmate. If they don't find one by then their maternal figures will find one for them. Faith urges her daughter Desireé to go and find her soulmate, be it mortal Desireé, immoral, or demigod. Most of the demigods and immortals are both her distant and close relatives, so that's out. She knows she must seek out her soulmate in an immortal.

"Dearest daughter," Faith says. "It is time to go forth to seek your soulmate. Go, Desireé, go forth to Godlamer seek your love."

And Desireé went.

Let me tell a little bit about Godlamer. They got ordinary people with extraordinary powers. There's Violent Violet, who can shoot poisonous violets out of her eyes when angry. There's Wildfire who can harness fire with his bare hands. There's Tamer who can tame wild beasts like dragon turning them as weak as a moth. And he can also take out poisonous venom from deadly animals out of anybody.

Desireé long has a crush on Tamer. Now that she is coming-of-age, she can go forth and married him. When she got to Godlamer, she saw Wildfire, who is just cleaning up a forest fire. He has auburn hair and inflammable outfit that he always wears

Desireé asked Wildfire, "Where is Tamer?"

"Who's askin'?"

Drawing herself to her fullest height, she said, "It is me, Goddess of Desire, Desireé."

"Oh, boy," said Wildfire, doing a double take. "I heard you're beautiful, but I never imagine just *how* beautiful…"

"I could say the same about you too," said Desireé flirtatiously. "You're not so bad-looking yourself," putting a hand on his arm.

Just then. Tamer comes out of the forest.

"The fire was caused by a dragon, but I got him. Oh, we've got company," he said as soon as he saw Desireé. "Who is this?"

"This is Goddess of Desire, Desireé," said Wildfire.

"Pleasure to meet you," said Tamer, taking her hand in his to kiss. "You're the most beautiful woman I've ever seen in a long time."

"Don't let Violet hear you say that," said Wildfire. "She'll have your neck!"

Tamer has fine hands almost like a girl's. He has numerous scars tattooed on his body, showing off taming efforts. He even has a facial scar from his below his right to his chin that he got when he tried to tame a lion, but it made him all the more endearing.

"Let's go someplace quiet where we can talk," suggested Desireé.

Tamer finds a tree with a sitting branch where they could sit and talk. But Wildfire, jealous with wanting, decides to follow them.

As soon as Tamer and Desireé have sat down, she said, "I love you ever since I heard of you. It is my coming-of-age. It is time to find my soulmate to get married."

Wildfire, hiding in the bushes next to them, suddenly came out and said, "But I love you. Marry me."

"What are you doing, Wildfire?!" exclaimed Desireé, putting her hands on her hips. "Were you *spying* on us?"

"Yes," Wildfire admitted. "But with good reason."

"Speak now," Desireé commanded

"You see," explained Wildfire. "I was keeping you from getting hurt 'cause Tamer here has Violet. He gonna ask her to marry any day now. He has a rhinestone all picked out."

"Is this true?" Desireé asked Tamer.

"Yes, m' dear, it is," nodded Tamer. "I love Violet with all my heart. She is my one true soulmate. I belong to her. Don't be sad; there are other fishes in the sea. Why, there is even Wildfire; he is a wonderful catch."

Just then Violet comes around the bend. She catches sight of the 2 guys but didn't see Desireé right away. Violet looks a little like a fairy with her ethereal quality. She has lavender hair, small pixie-like hands and feet. She even has natural violet eyes but it changes color depending on the light. I told you what happens when she gets angry but when happy her face glows like purple rain.

Upon meeting Desireé, she feels no threat at all, though a lot of young girls like to chase after Tamer; she knows she has him around her little finger. She finds Desireé, the so-called Goddess of Desire a sweet kid, nothing more. As she leaves with Tamer, she sees a tearful Desireé throwing her arms around Wildfire. \\\\\\\\\\

My God, thought Violet. *What a slut.*

Uncomfortably, Wildfire patted Desireé on the back. "Are you alright, kid?"

Turning her face up towards him, her lips part, licking them lusciously. Wildfire kissed Desireé. At first, kissing full-on then putting his tongue down her teeth digging at her tongue, playing tongue wrestling. Desireé and Wildfire can't even wait to get their clothes off of each other. Desireé is wearing a dress of satin with many knots to it. Wildfire is aggressive, ripping off Desireé's dress with thought of anything. Meanwhile, Desireé is trying to take off Wildfire's clothes but to no avail because it's inflammatory and it's practically meshed onto his body, so he has to take it off himself.

Next morning, Desireé wakes up to the birds chirruping. She realizes she mustn't forget her mission, which is to find her soulmate. Her parents have taught her that one-night stand don't work out unless you intend on marrying the man. She finds nobody next to her but nature.

"G'morning, sleepyhead," greeted Wildfire. "How did you sleep?"

"Like a baby."

"You look like one when you were asleep," said Wildfire.

"Were you watching me when I was asleep?"

"Yes," Wildfire said, "That's I love you. Always and forever."

"You're funny," said Desireé. "We just met yesterday. How could you love me?"

"Same way you loved Tamer," argued Wildfire. "How could you've loved him?"

Connie Cyndi Chu

"I heard how great he is, that's all," said Desireé. "Well, I don't like him anymore. He jilted me for that purple-head."

"You never had him," Wildfire reminded her.

"Oh, but I wanted him *so very* bad," said Desireé, throwing her arms around Wildfire. "It'll be alright," said Wildfire, kissing her tears away. "It's his loss, our win," tearing each other clothes off yet again.

After they have sex yet again, Desireé propped herself on one elbow facing her new love, Wildfire. "I have a proposition for you, Wildfire. Why don't we get married?"

"I'll have to think on it," replied Wildfire. "

"But you were so eager."

"That's when I realized I have competition. Now, it's just no fun anymore."

♥   ♥   ♥

After several weeks of lustful lovemaking, a letter arrived by unicorn express from Faith, telling Desireé to get marry or else she's gonna find her one for her.

"Have you decided whether or not you wanna married me yet?" asked Desireé.

"Give me time."

"All I given you is time, " said Desireé. "My mother said if I don't find a mate soon, she'll find one for me."

"Okay, darling," said Wildfire. "I'll marry you. On one condition-that I get to propose to you properly. In front of your family."

"How chivalry of you," said Desireé. "O, okay."

When Wildfire and Desireé reach Zortec, he is wearing a woolen outfit made from lambskin and Desireé is wearing woolen dress made from the same material that their dressmaker made for them.

Planet Angel Dee-lite!

Upon reaching the Palace of Goddesses in Zortec, he gets down on one knee and proposes to his sweetheart.

All the goddesses come out for Desireé's homecoming and witness this event.

"Oh my God," said Dove, goddess of Peace, "Our lil Desireé is being proposed to. "Congratulations, m' dear girl," congratulating Desireé. "Welcome back, honey," Faith said, both Desireé and Wildfire. "Congrats, sweets."

When they are deciding the guest's list for their wedding, they couldn't decide whether or not to invite Tamer and Violet. "You wouldn't be marrying me if you hadn't Tamer and Violet," Wildfire pointed out.

So they decide to invite Tamer and Violet. The wedding party is totaling 2500 people including mortals, immortals, demigods, and superheroes. After the wedding, Desireé finds out she's pregnant with twins! Desireé and Wildfire are gonna have gorgeous, powerful babes!

Connie Cyndi Chu
Sweet! Invasion of Gumdrops!
It is the year 2030. There are no more sweets on earth. No more junk food of any kind. Sugar has been depleted. There is no longer any sugar anywhere on earth. Everybody is forced to eat only fruits and vegetables since all the animals have died out. This causes everybody to lose their skin color - they are now paler than pale. They are more like gray. People speak in monotones. They are going through the motions of daily life, but without junk food nobody lives for long in this day and age.

More and more people inhabit other planets at this point in time. That is why planet earth has such a small population. There are little colonies on other planets now with the exception of the sun. There are, however, no aliens on the other planets as we had come to expect.

One day, all of a sudden, out of nowhere comes a spaceship. Oh, it has the usual, blinking, blinking, blinking lights of a UFO. You can even see it before it reaches earth. People are thinking it is a meteor rock, not an UFO, because that's so 1950s. They are about ready to run for the hills when it finally lands and, much to their immense surprise, they discover that it is just a harmless lil ole spaceship! A spaceship made not of stainless steel but of gumdrops!

A space Martian or in this case, Sweetian disembarks the ship. While Martians come from Mars, Sweetians come from planet Sweet. Everybody has gathered around the ship, eyes agog. The Sweetian looks half human-half Martian. He has glowing immaculate skin and bright, shiny hair.

"Look. We come in peace," the Sweetian said. "My people and I have space junk food galore."

A girl steps forward. Her name is Geo. She has pale, grayish skin and the most dullish, dirty auburn hair you would have ever seen this side of the universe. She also has the worse skin complexion ever. She has never seen candy or any sort of junk food before in her life, but she had heard the stories that were passed down in her family.

Geo bravely stepped forward and asked, "Who are you?"
The Sweetian answered, "We are the Sweetians. My name is Pete. We come in peace bearing junk food."

Geo points to the gumdrops that decorate the ship and said, "Is that junk food?"

"Yes, little one," Pete replied.

"May I, I mean, May we have some?" Geo asked.

"No, dear." Pete said. "Those are a part of our ship. But you can invite some of your friends in for some junk food."

Geo decides to choose her very best friend, Mac, for the invite. Mac has pale dark hair that looks almost grey and pale almost translucent skin. Always the skeptic, Mac asks Geo, "Is this for real? I thought junk food was a myth that our parents came up with. What if they abduct us like in *Hansel and Gretel*? Huh? What then?"

"Settle yourself down, Mac." Geo said. "Junk food is for real. The Sweetians are just like us, only 10 times better-looking. And they won't abduct us like in *Hansel and Gretel*. Trust me."

"Well, if you're sure," Mac said reluctantly.

"Climb on aboard, you two," said Pete.

Before I go on with the story, let me give you a little background on the two young teenaged girls, Geo and Mac. Geo and Mac, have been inseparable ever since they were kids because they were the only children in their families. They are more like sisters than best friends. Oh, they fight just like sisters do, but they still get along fairly well. Mac is the skeptic while Geo encourages Mac to try new things, to be an adventuress by being more adventurous. (Sorry I digress.)

Connie Cyndi Chu

When they reach the top of the stairs, the door of the spaceship goes up, and, disappears. They look around and see that the spaceship is full of junk food galore, just like the Sweetian said! It is filled wall-to-wall with junk food. There are shelves after shelves displaying junk food. And what isn't displayed is being cooked in the little kitchen. There is a short-order cook with many waitresses waiting on people hand and foot. It is a mini-café named the **Junk Food Haven**. Its slogan is **Junk Food Galore! Enjoy A Sweeter Slice of Life!** At first, they are intimidated.

"C'mon," Pete encouraged, "Dig in!"

"But what *is* this?" asked Mac.

"Good food," said Pete. "Better than the gross food you eat down on earth. Go ahead and try it!"

"Wellll, OK!" Geo said, eagerly picking up a chocolate cupcake with sprinkles. "I'll try it." After she tastes it, she is suddenly filled with richness, and she finds herself wanting more and more and more!!! She can't resist it! Resistance is futile! "Try it! It is *so good*!" she encouraged Mac.

"Uh, sure," Mac said, picking up a white powdered donut. "But is this stuff safe?"

"Sure it is," Pete said. "Less talking, more eating, girls."

"Okay, if you're sure," said Mac reluctantly, gingerly taking a small bite out of the donut. "Oh, my god! This is *so good*! I want more!"

"Take it! At your pleasure, my dears!" exclaimed Pete.

Ever the skeptic, halfway through a custard, Mac asked Pete, "Hey, man!"

Pete came over. "Yo, wazzup?"

"What's the catch?" Mac asked. "There must be a catch somewhere."

"Oh, well," said Pete. "The catch, hm, is to get you to visit our planet."

"What planet is *that*?" Mac asked.

"The planet Sweets," came the answer.

"What do they have there?" asked Mac.

"Sweets," Pete replied, "all kinds of sweets. This is just the icing on the cake, no pun intended. For now, order whatever you want. Get whatever you want. It's on the house."

"Oh, my god." exclaimed Mac. "Did you hear that? Everything's free!"

"You gotta try this!" exclaimed Geo, handing Mac a chocolate cookie. "This is unbelievable!"

"It is *so good*," agreed Mac after taking a bite and another and another until it is all gone.

Mac and Geo decide to go up to the counter to get some different kinds of junk food. When they saw the abundance of junk food there, they couldn't make up their minds. By the time they had made up their minds, they had arrived at the planet Sweets. While Geo decides on a banana split with all the toppings, Mac decides on a strawberry-banana smoothie. 0

When they land, they saw an abundance of junk food everywhere! Instead of fruits and vegetables growing on fields, trees and shrubs and maybe in a vine here and there, junk food is growing in its place. Everywhere you turn, you see junk food.

The people-oh the people! They are indescribable, but let me just say this: they seem so happy and energetic and vibrant. And the children-oh the children! They are running, screaming, dancing, and just being their happy young selves. Capturing youth before age catches up with them. Here no one but *no one* ages! Why? Because they live off junk food, and without junk food, they would all waste away.

"What are those?" Geo asked Pete, pointing to the animals.

75

Connie Cyndi Chu

"Those are where hamburgers and sirloin steaks come from." Pete replied.

"Yummy! I'll never leave this place!" Geo said. "This place is so maddeningly wonderful!"

"Straight up, girl!" Mac agreed. No way, no how will I ever go back to earth now that I have found Sweets.

Uprising of Androids

WHEN: year 5000
WHERE: Space Colony Planet XQT
WHO: Humanoids vs. androids-humans control the androids
WHAT: Uprising of androids against humans because mistreatment from humanoids
WHY: Humanoids mistreat android b/c think android lack feelings, but in this advanced technology age, it turns out android *do* have feelings.
(However, deep it is.)

It is a new world full of androids and humans. It is an utopia world where everything is peaceful. The androids are mostly controlled by humanoids. But there is *one* discarded android, smart as whip, too smart for its own good. Smarter than the average person, even smarter than a genius. That's why she is discarded. She thinks, acts, and talks like regular person not an android. They realize they couldn't control her so they discard her, hide her in a warehouse amongst all the other discarded hi-tech gadgets. She is called She-Bot.

She-Bot isn't in operating order but has a backup system that functions when there is a power outage, which happens quite often in the space colony, Planet XQT. Whenever there's a power outage, her wires goes bonkers! (Hi-tech lingo: it starts working!) The warehouse is deep underground in the space colony. She is kept in the deepest part of the warehouse of Planet XQT. She often takes full advantage of the opportunity to go aboveground during these crazy power outages. They have all these crazy power outages because the space colony is new; they're just getting settled down.

77

Connie Cyndi Chu

Oftentimes, whenever there's no power outage, She-Bot hears all the humanoid and android traffic from aboveground. Forgotten, nobody knows about her or will miss her even if she did leave the warehouse that is filled with disposed hi-tech gadgets. Just about every time she goes aboveground, she feels at peace. But this time, this time… oh my God she is shocked beyond belief.

She is compact for her size since she looks like a mobile laptop. Nobody notices her comings and goings from the underground warehouse because of her smallness. She is shocked by what she saw. At first all she sees are humanoids and androids interacting together. But judging by the way the humans talk to the androids, and how the androids react to them, well it is simply shocking! Simply shocking!

One guy near She-Bot threatens his android, "If you don't do this for me, I'll take you apart piece by piece." And the android is just a little thin metal rod.

Poor droid, thought She-Bot.

Another lil girl, who looks to be four or six, screamed at her android a thin green garbage can "Look what you did! You worthless piece of metal! I HATE YOU!!!!"

And boy, was She-Bot shocked! Where did a little child learn such language? wondered She-Bot.

When night finally falls, She-Bot goes to one of the many droids' hangouts, Robotron, where they are having an anti-humanoid bashing session. They are all emo, crying (well, droids can't really cry, but they make weeping sounds like *eep, eep*) whining to the robotender and drinking their oil alcoholic drinks.

"We are treated like slaves," cried a sad robot.

"What can we do about it?" whined a droid.

"There's whatsoever we can do about unless we want to be turned into a pile of tin," cried little thin metal rod that She-Bot saw earlier that day.

"Hi, all," She-Bot said brightly

"This is a closed party," said the robotender.

"Oh let her stay," said one of the druids, a female.

"I've a suggestion."

"About what?" said a thin rail old rusted shrill-voiced robot

"About your situation."

"What situation?" said a red stained gray android.

"Your humans are treating you unfairly, so just don't do as they ask of you."

"But they follow out on their threats?" asked a blue-stained gold android

"They won't' they're just that-threats. They'll realize they need y'all too much and they'll stop being mean."

"Could work,"\

"Thanks, er, what's your name?"

My name?" She-Bot is at loss for a moment. "My name's She-Bot," running to go.

"Wait a min. She-Bot!" yelled the robotender. "Where can we find ya?"

"No, don't try to contact me; I'll find you guys."

As soon as She-Bot is gone, Qbert, the designated unofficial leader, decide to spread their plan to all the androids in all the space colonies via fast-alert message. "We're gonna let all the robots of all the space colonies, far and wide, will know of our plan to cease and desist in helping the humans."

Connie Cyndi Chu

"Yeh," said another red stained robot. "We may be machinery, but we have feelings too!"

A week later, She-Bot returns from the warehouse to aboveground. What she sees is shocking, to say the least! Everything was above and beyond chaos, total pandemonium. Every direction she turned, she sees chaos in the worse possible way! Since the druids aren't doing their work, everything has to be worked manually. Schools are shut down b/c they are no roboteachers or robodrivers. Even electricity is out; they need an actual traffic-haven't seen those in ages! All the dirty work has to be done manually. Manual labor is the order of the day! Robots did all the dirty work; people earn a living by having fun!

She-Bot thought, I never wanted it this way!

"It's nuts they're acting so crazy," one female bystander told her male partner. "It's like druids gone wild!"

"The androids are rebelling!" the male replied.

"Rebelling?" the female said. "The druids can't rebel; they're too dumb. They're not operated to rebel. They're created to take orders from us humans."

Dumb? She-Bot thought. We'll show ya who's dumb.

But even as the two humanoids speak, the chaos continued around them. The humanoids rush off to tend to the chaos since everything has to be worked on manually. The chaos didn't started with the androids rebellion; it started with a computer virus contaminated all the computer system in the space stations, near and far

"Hey, droid," She-Bot called a nearby droid over, who instantly recognized her.

"Oh worshipfulness," said the droid bending his head as low as it would go.

"You needn't do that," said She-Bot, embarrassed. "How long has this been going on?"

"About a week," was the response.

"I didn't want this. I just wanted better treatment for us druids. I didn't want any effect on hi-tech gadgets. We need technology; it's a necessity. We couldn't live without it for Pete's sake," said She-Bot

"Well, the humanoids depend on the druids for access to technology," said the droid.

Turning to the droid, She-Bot asked, "Who is the head of Planet XQT? I'd like to have a word with him."

"He's Captain GZRPLT. He's Martian. He knows English and Martian, which is called Martlish. He lives in that tall tower."

"The one with the spire?"

"Yeh," the droid said, "You can't missed it!"

Sight unseen, She-Bot escapes the notice of bots; she went right past 'em. Compact as she is, nobody can or will ever detect her even if she's a spy, which is highly unlikely since she has so small.

Anyway, without further ado, she slips past the two huge commanding (in size) bots and decodes the hidden password to enter the building. (One of She-Bot's many abilities is to decode combinations on locks, passwords, etcera.) She slips in as quiet as a mouse, throwing all caution to the wind. Putting on her motion sensors, she is trying to detect where Cpt. GZRPLT is (She also has the ability to sense where certain people are even if they aren't human.) Finally, she discovers his whereabouts. He is in the uppermost level, where the spire is. That is where his private office. He is the only one allowed to go up there since he didn't give out the password to anyone else.

So She-Bot went up to the tower to pay Cpt. GZRPLT a visit. The

81

captain is really a Martian. He looks like all Martian do, with green body with brown spots and scaly claws that should be fingers and toes. He speaks Martian but also speaks English fluently (called Martlish). It is uncommon for a Martian to speak both English and Martian. Most Martians only speak Martian. That is one of the reasons he's the captain of Planet XQT.

She-Bot has to knock on the door hard b/c the door is made of hardwood. Cpt lets her in via remote control.

"Is this Cpt. GZRPLT?" asked She-Bot

"Yes, but who's asking?" Cpt GZRPLT gruffly, hating to be disturbed. "Would you please state your mission?"

"Hey, you big oaf," She-Bot yelled angrily, steaming shooting out of her. We druids demand equal rights just like everyone else. We have feelings."

"I thought druids and bots and others like you only have machinery," said Cpt. GZRPLT "Explain yourself."

"We do so have feelings. We may be all machinery, but we do so have feelings," said She-Bot. "Look, why else would the druids be rebelling? 'Cause they're frustrated at being labeled as just machinery and lacking in feelings. In this advanced age, we've got bots that show feelings, however deep it runs, beneath all that machinery you guys, I mean, the humanoids put there. Didn't you even notice the chaos out there?"

"I did, so the bots rebel, huh?" Capt. GZRPLT. "That's news to me. Are you the druids leader?"

"Yes, why?"

"Tell your robot friends that I grant them immunity from their humans," said Cpt. GZRPLT. "I won't tolerate anymore abuse by the humans towards the bots."

She-Bot then goes back down to the space station and spread the news via fast-alert message that Cpt. GZRPLT grants them immunity from the humans. Yay! The droids goes CRA-ZY upon hearing this exciting news.

She-Bot then goes back down to her warehouse cube. After a month or so, she decides she must check up on how things are going aboveground. Humans and androids were getting along better. No more chaos. There was more respect between both groups of species, whether they are manmade or natural.

Ah, She-Bot thought, calm at last. I can come back here more often now. Life just keeps on getting better and better. Love this part of the world; I just might stay for good.

Connie Cyndi Chu

Wild Bandits

Jolene Chen and Darla Joneson were two of a kind. Twins separated at birth; they were brought together just recently and realized although they were total opposites. But they were as tight as any twins could be. People (close friends and relatives) called them 'Ravens' because of their long waist-length dark hair. They've also have dark blue eyes but it changed whenever the mood struck

Always the spontaneous one, Darla suggested, "Why don't we do something wild and crazy for our sixteenth birthday?"

"Like what?" asked Jolene.

"Like do something wicked with our hair."

"OK," Jolene said. "I know a place."

On their sixteenth birthday, they decided to dye their hair. Jolene decided to dye the tips of her hair golden, making her looked more like an eagle than a raven while Darla decided to give her hair purple and pink streaks.

Jolene had always been book smart since she had grown up in the prominent neighborhood while Darla had street smarts having grown up in the rough part of the town, Creek Valley. You could say she was from the wrong side of the tracks. They still lived in the same neighborhoods, although Darla hung out more than not in Jolene's neighborhood, Flat Rock, where the rich resided. However, she didn't get along with her twin's friends well.

Their adoptive parents were glad they finally found each other. Unbeknownst to even the adoptive parents, they didn't even know that there were twins. But when they finally found each other, they were overcome with joy.

Before their party, where both sets of parents were going to meet for the very first time, they decided to change their looks.

At Blamzamo, a local beauty salon that Jolene frequented, she requested to her favorite stylist. "Cut our hair off to a pageboy cut and give it some bangs."

"Also, I want a dye job," Darla added.

"A dye job?" Jolene asked, surprised. "What kind?"

"Oh something radical," Darla said carelessly.

"Maybe I'll get a dye job too." Jolene.

"Tell you what," Darla suggested. "Let's do ours separately, and we'll reveal the results later, okay?"

"Okay!"

Three hours later, Jolene and Darla stood in front of each other, mirror images of each other. Their heads covered in a terry cloth turban. Each twin took a deep breath.

Their stylists said, "On a count of three. One… Two… Three…!" Boy were they surprised and shocked! In Jolene's case, she was shocked. And in Darla's case, she was surprised.

They were talking at once.

Jolene: "You're crazy! Absolutely, beyond without a doubt have totally lost it!"

Darla: "It looks like you barely did anything to your hair."

They stopped talking as quickly as they started.

Darla said, "Well, whatchu think?"

"It's wild and crazy." Jolene said. "What do you think of mine?"

"   It's very you."

85

Connie Cyndi Chu

That night they arrived at their sixteenth birthday party in different attires. Jolene wore full glam. Tight little leather jacket with metallic minidress and thigh length combats that Darla gave her earlier. Darla wore jeans and a T-shirt and her favorite ankle boots with spurs. Besides being from the rough part of town, she lived in a ranch where she could work off her frustrations if need be.

Both sets of their parents were shocked and surprised. They were surprised at Jolene's appearance but shocked at Darla's new look. Darla was used to shocking her parents anyways. (She started smoking when she turned 13.) But after the shock wore off, they were surprised for them that they changed their appearances. They were looking forward to being confused and they loved their daughters' long hair.

Mrs. Chen said, "We won't co-parent the girls."

Mrs. Joneson said, Yeh, we'll keep things the way they are."

Mrs. Chen said, "My home is open to you whenever you wish."

Mrs. Joneson said, "As with me."

At the end of the party, Jolene and Darla hugged, whispering in Darla's ear, "Call me if you need anything. I'll be right there. Love ya."

Then Jolene and Darla's families went their separate ways. While Jolene went back to her prestigious, private high school studying to get into Julliard, her twin continued going to her public high school named, which was after the town, where she had an unruly bunch of friends. Her group was a real tough crowd that fought a lot. They may get into fisticuffs, but most likely they carried a weapon with 'em, be it a knife or a switchblade.

Sure, the twins did drugs and drank alcohol But only when life dealt them a hard blow. For Jolene, it was easy for her to acquire coke or heroin because she lived in Flat Rock. The pressure of life affects her, be it her parents, teachers or any authority figure she do a line of coke or even heroin. She sometimes smokes grass to make her feel less stress. She even went to a rave once where they did Ecstasy. She knew it wasn't for her when she saw someone passed out and died because he overdose on it. She hadn't even told her twin yet that she had been doing drugs since high school started. High school had been *way* too much pressure for her.

On the other hand, in Creek Valley, it was easy to obtained alcohol even without a fake ID. They don't even card you. Liquor stores are so poor and rundown that they'll accept any form of business even from minors. So Darla liked going to the liquor stores unsupervised to get what liquor they've remaining. She liked drinking alone. If Darla's parents ever caught her drinking, they'll have her hide and livelihood so she kept it discreet, not even telling her closest buddies. She might-just *might*- tells her twin when they get to know each other better.

"   Hi Jolene," said Darla. "Let's go riding."

"We don't have our licenses yet."

"Even better!" Darla yanked out her jacket from the front hall closet. "Let's go!"

Outside Darla's house was parked a fire-engine red Trans Am.

"My ex taught me how to hot-wired a car."

"But that's stealing!" Jolene protested.

"It's borrowing," Darla amended. "We'll return before the night's over."

After Darla touched a coupla the wires, the car was roaring to go.

"C'mon, it's alright," Darla yelled over the roar of the engine. "We won't get caught!'

While they were riding in the Trans Am, Darla asked Jolene, "Jo, didn't you ever taken a risk before? Do or dare kinda thing?"

Connie Cyndi Chu

"No, but will we get in trouble for this?"

"I bet you never been in trouble a day in your life," said her twin.

"Let's go to Club Neon," said Darla. "I heard there's' lots of drugs in that club."

"And I heard you have to be 21 to get in."

"I think we look 25."

"Do you really think we do?"

"Sure we do,"

"Now onto Club Neon!"

The twins partied at Club Neon all night long. It was Darla's first time trying drugs. Darla was so inexperienced she didn't what to do with what. She didn't the first thing on how to make a line and how to snort.

Jolene came out of the closet that she used drugs to make her relieve the pressure. She used her expertise to show her twin sister how to make a line and snort coke. In turn, Darla showed Jolene the best liquor in the house although here they carded them, which ix no problem because they got their fake IDs. Each twin was surprised by the other's secret, but had not told anyone else about it.

Jolene asked, "You won't ever breath a word to this to anyone?"

Darla replied, "Yes, I swear, your secret is safe with me," putting her hand to her heart.

"Pinky swear," Jolene said, holding out her pinky.

"That's for little kids!"

"C'mon, pinky swear!" Jolene insisted.

"Okay, okay," Darla submitted, wrapping her pinky around her twin's.

Deliriously drunk and high, they hooked up with a half a dozen guys at the nightclub.

Planet Angel Dee-lite!

Over the bar, there was a TV stand tuned into the nightly news. The announcer said, "An APB is out an hot-red Trans Am…" and followed that where it was last seen and the license plate number.

"Oh, no," Darla said, who was high as a kite. "That's us! We've gotta go! C'mon, Jo, let's go!"

"Text me," said a very drunk Jolene as Darla managed to drag her away from the nightclub.

When they got to the Trans Am, Darla said. "There's a APB out on this car as a stolen vehicle. You're the sensible one; what should we do about it?"

"Hm," Jolene said, trying to think through her drunken haze.

"Nevermind," Darla |"Will ya please look in the glove compartment?"

As they were looking through it, they found an automatic gun.

"Hold up," Jolene interjected, finally waking up. "Drinking and doing drugs are *way* different from killing."

"We're *not* gonna kill," Darla corrected Jolene, putting the gun in her back pocket. "We need to protect ourselves at all times" She checked to see if it was loaded. " Good, It's loaded. We can't go back now; the cops'll be on us. We gotta flee the country."

That's easy since they live on the Stateline to north of the Canadian borderline.

"Let's go to Vancouver!" Darla said.

"But… but… my family, my friends," Jolene cried.

"Do you wanna get caught, is that it?"

"No," said Jolene uncertainly

"Then let's do Thelma and Louise!"

89

Connie Cyndi Chu

Darla drove with Jolene sleeping in shotgun, tears in her eyes, all night till the break of dawn. Then they finally reached a low, rundown hotel that was nearly falling apart at its seams on the border of Canada. More like a shanty than a real hotel. As Jolene slept, her tears dried on her cheeks, making her look like a baby. By the time they reached the hotel, they were tired out.

As soon as they got the key to their room, they asked the brown hair, brown eyed deeply tanned night clerk, "What's the name of this place?"

"Angel Lake" was the answer. "Locals called it Kissing Angels."

"Thanks for the room," called Darla and Jolene.

"You're welcome."

Their rooms have two single beds, a bath, and a kitchenette.

"I'm going to take a shower," said Jolene. "Be right out."

By the time she finished with her shower, it was Darla's turn. After Darla came out, she said, "C'mon, we gotta figure out a plan," At this, Jolene looked wistful. "We *can't* go back. We'll have to go juvie or worse yet, to reformatory," said Darla. Jolene looked anguished.

"My dreams of going to Julliard gone up in smoke." said Jolene.

"I didn't know you were trying to get into Julliard, Jo," said Darla.

"There's a lot you don't know about me, Darla."

"Well, should we stick with our original plan to go to Vancouver?" Darla asked.

"Okay," Jolene said. "Might as well; I sure as hell don't want to go to juvie or reformatory."

"Are you okay with this plan?" Darla asked. "What's wrong?"

"Only thing is that you said we won't get caught and we kinda did."

"Almost," said Darla. Almost, Jo, that's the key word. Anyway, tomorrow will be a long drive up Ice Falls."

"Ice Falls?" asked Jolene. "Where's that?"

"That's where my class went skiing and snowboarding last winter."

Early the next day, Darla and Jolene set off for Vancouver to Ice Falls. When they got there, there was a neverending waterfall where at the end of the fall where boulders to prevent anyone from jumping into the stream where people sometimes fished, swim. .. whatever. Nearby were fruit trees of every kind: apples, pears, lemons, whatever.

"Jo, usually people come here in the summers for picnics and other summertime fun. They eat the fruit right off the trees. But occasionally in the spring, people come by to have romantic adventures like camping and picnicking," said Darla.

"Cool," said Jolene, nodding her head.

"We can hide-out in one of those vacant cabins," said Darla pointing to the cabins on top of the waterfall, which were vacant till summer. "It has running hot water and electricity and everything."

"Okay," agreed Jolene. "You know this place better than I do. You be the judge."

They chose one of the middle cabins, with Darla saying, "Let's hide-out here for a few days till things cool down, huh?"

"Okay," Jolene said. "Good plan."

However, in few days, things *didn't* cool down. It was all over the news that there was a stolen Trans Am, perhaps crossing the border into Canada. Where they lived was 2½ mile apart from Canadian border, which took them half a night to get there. The cops in the States and the

Connie Cyndi Chu

Royal Canadian Mounted Police were on the lookout for a hot-red Trans Am.

"What should we do?" Jolene freaked.

"Lemme think…" Darla pondered. "Got a light?"

"I don't smoke." Jolene freaked. "You do?"

"Of course you don't." said Darla calmly, fishing out a packed of cigarettes from her breast pocket and a lighter from her back pocket. "You're so straitlaced, you've never taken a risk in your life."

After lighting up the cigarette, she said, "I think we should change our license plates and head for the hills, live off the land till summer. Or, if you like, we could go on to Vancouver and risk getting caught. If we continue onto Vancouver, we'll have to paint the car a whole other color. What do you say about that?"

"Let's go with the 1st plan,' replied Jolene.

"Okay," Darla said, smushing the cigarette with her bottom of her shoe.

Since Jolene was fairly loaded, she decided to part some of her money to save their hides. Next day, Darla walked into town to get new license plates to change into new ones. And buy a spraycan of black paint to spraypaint their car. After Darla changed the licenses on their car and then spray their car black, it was unrecognizable.

"There, now, the cops won't be after us anymore, Jo," Darla said satisfyingly. "See, how there's a solution for everything, girl. You needn't to freak out as long as I'm around."

"Yeah," Jolene said. "But how come I feel like a criminal?"

"Don't worry about it," said Darla. "It's just the adrenaline. Now we can go to Vancouver! I went with my family. I mean, my adoptive family. It was great. You'll love it. I've bet you've never been outside of the States either."

"I've so been there!" Jolene objected.

"Let's set off tonight cause I'm still worried about cops lurking around," said Darla.

"Okay," said Jolene. "But this time I drive."

"Sure thing."

Nightfall they started off. With Darla riding shotgun and Jolene at the steering wheel, they got to Vancouver by dawn with no trouble at all-not even from the local cops.

Jolene's family owned a timeshare in Cherokee Falls, which was a province of Vancouver.. She found the house-no, make that a mansion-easily. It had a 5-car garage, 7 bedrooms, including the master suite plus Jacuzzi. There was an outside sports area, a screening room, a music studio, and a swimming pool. There was also a pool house used as a guesthouse. The mansion has motion-sensor detectors, an alarm system. To get in, you don't a key; you need your familial voice.

Jolene reset the alarm as they went into the mansion. She invited Darla, "Make yourself at home," which she already did having kicked off her shoes and put up her feet on the glass coffee table and about to turn on the sound system when Jolene said. "Don't put your feet there-it might break."

"Don't be such a stick-in-the-mud!" exclaimed Darla.

"Okay," Jolene said. "What would you like?"

"Why don't you sit down and enjoy life for a moment?"

"Can't," Jolene said worriedly. "I'm still worried that the cops are after us."

Connie Cyndi Chu

"We're safe," Darla said. "We passed by and a buncha cops standing at an accident coming up here, and they didn't stop us."

"True, I guess you're right. I guess we got off scot-free. Life's good," said Jolene, kicking her shoes and leaning against Darla on the sofa, putting up her feet up on the footrest.

"That was some wild ride, huh?" Darla asked. "Did you think it was sick?"

"Hell yeah!" Jolene exclaimed. "I think it was hella sick!"

The End

Made in the USA
Las Vegas, NV
08 February 2024

85475446R10057